A Children's Game . . .

Mark Hardin watched the thug emerge from the rows of cars and followed his progress, keeping Redfield over the sights of his MatchMaster pistol. The howling siren grew louder and the hood suddenly bolted into the open.

Mark aimed carefully and squeezed the trigger.

The Safari Arms blaster boomed and the .45 caliber projectile sliced through the air and found exactly the target the Penetrator wanted. The bullet hit Redfield in the left thigh, pierced flesh and muscle and snapped the bone beneath like a dry tree branch struck by lightning.

The hitman cried out in surprise and pain. Redfield fell to the pavement as though slapped down by an invisible giant's hand. He sprawled on his belly and the Beretta flew from his grasp to skid ten feet beyond the killer's reach.

"Tag," Mark said, pleased that he'd been able to take one of the hoods alive. "You're it."

. . . with a Deadly Twist

THE PENETRATOR SERIES:

No. 51

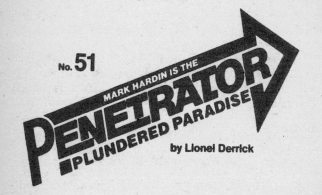

MARK HARDIN IS THE

PENETRATOR

PLUNDERED PARADISE

by Lionel Derrick

PINNACLE BOOKS **NEW YORK**

PENETRATOR 51: PLUNDERED PARADISE

Copyright © 1983 by Pinnacle Books, Inc.

An original Pinnacle Books edition, published for the first time anywhere.

First printing, July, 1983

Special Acknowledgement: Mark Roberts

ISBN: 0-523-41736-5

Cover illustration by George Wilson

Printed in the United States of America

PINNACLE BOOKS, INC.
1430 Broadway
New York, New York 10018

This one is for two fine friends,
Sandy and Elizabeth Brygider.
Best to you always.

PLUNDERED PARADISE

1

S. O. S.

"May as well give it up," Captain Solomon Wakely muttered to himself. His eyes felt grainy from staring into the blank gray wall.

The skipper of *Neptune's Dream* spun the big wooden wheel of the sturdy fishing trawler a few points to starboard and let the vessel swing with the tide. With the other hand he raised a cup of rum-laced coffee to his mouth and smacked his lips in appreciation. Sea air can be chilly at night, he reminded himself, especially when fog and age have set in. Wakely's old turtleneck sweater and Navy peacoat weren't enough to combat the clammy coldness that seemed to seep through his skin to pierce the very marrow of his bones. A man needs something warm inside himself as well and rum was a tradition among men of the sea. Who was Solomon Wakely to argue with such a fine, time-honored practice?

Wakely had spent most of his sixty-three years at sea. His face had been scored and lined by exposure to the elements and his physique remained lean and well-muscled. Hard work had been his forte since childhood and the sea had indeed been his mistress. Wakely certainly lived his chosen role. An iron-gray beard decorated his lantern jaw and he seldom removed his battered captain's cap. He was an old sea dog, an anachronism of a romantic time long past.

Solomon Wakely remembered the old days when he could haul in a fine catch of fish in his nets and make a decent living at his trade. Those days had gone and so had the large catches of the past. Pollution had killed off some fish and the big commercial purse seines systematically scooped up the remaining schools of tuna and mackerel.

The big outfits were too thorough in Wakely's opinion. He had never caught an entire school of fish with *his* nets. Always there were plenty left to repopulate for the following year. Now, most canneries were run by corporations that couldn't care less about the sea or the balance of nature, so long as they made a profit. Wakely had secretly cheered the Mexican *Guardia Costal* when they'd seized U.S. tuna boats a few years ago.

Yet Wakely couldn't blame his lack of success on anyone but himself. He realized that he should have taken advantage of his younger years of plenty and invested money instead of spending it on strong drink and loose women. He'd been too busy playing sailor even then. He smiled bitterly, recalling the main reason he'd been so cavalier with his money for the last thirty-five years.

He'd listened to all those doomsayers after World War Two. Atom bombs would destroy the world, they said. Nuclear war with the Russians always seemed to be right around the corner, so why save for a future that could suddenly end when Washington and Moscow decided to hurl missiles at each other?

Armageddon hadn't arrived and Wakely almost wished it had. Living on Social Security checks or worse, in a state-owned nursing home for the aged, frightened him far more than simple global destruction.

"Captain!" Al Fontaine exclaimed, thrusting his round, beet-red face through the doorway of the small weather bridge. "There's a light flashin' out there, off the port bow, sir."

Wakely turned to stare at Fontaine. His first mate ressembled a pug-faced dog with sad, blue eyes. The captain knew Al wasn't very bright, but he wasn't inclined to have hallucinations either.

"We're off the coast of Baja California," Wakely commented. "Could be another boat out there even in this weather. Does she appear to be coming toward us?"

"No, sir," Fontaine answered. "But I think she's flashin' a message to us in Morse Code. Told Jim and he went forward to give a look-see."

Wakely nodded. "Take the wheel, Al. Hold her on one-five-zero."

The captain stepped onto the deck. He smelled the familiar, biting salt tang of the sea, combined with the stench of fish slime from the holds below. He could see little of his surroundings due to the fog. Dense gray mist filled the night in thick, undulating layers, intermittently separated by narrow bands of stygian blackness. It blotted out the sky and covered the ocean. It clung to *Neptune's Dream* like the sucker discs of a giant squid.

Wakely trembled under the clammy embrace.

Yet the physical effects of the fog had little to do with the cold tremor that crept along his spine. Taking his boat out on such a night had been only marginally risky. He'd hoped to haul in a substantial catch before the commercial fleets set to work. Radar and the RDF (Radio Direction Finder) would keep a boat from running ashore or prevent a collision, but they wouldn't lay nets. He thought he'd have the sea to himself. Somehow, though, the thought of a ship in distress disturbed him. Outside the physical hazards of rendering assistance in these weather conditions, the possibility of it being real seemed ominous. With a final shudder he dismissed his mood as the foolishness of old age.

"Captain?"

The voice of Jim Boggs came from one of two vaguely humanoid shapes in the swirling fog.

"I'm coming," Wakely replied, trying to ignore his apprehension.

Boggs and the other shadow, Frank Tell, stood near the bow by the railing, watching a white light that blinked feebly in the thick, gray mass. Dot, dot, dot—dash, dash, dash—dot, dot, dot.

"S.O.S.," Wakely remarked, reading the signal.

"Yes, sir," Boggs nodded. He was a twenty-three year old Navy veteran who'd joined Wakely's crew because he'd learned to love the sea although he despised the military. He held an ACR/4F "Firefly" rescue light in his hand. "Should I reply to their distress call?"

"Of course," Wakely snapped with irritation. No man of the sea would ignore a plea for help from a vessel in trouble. However, he realized, Boggs was following proper procedure by leaving the decision for the captain to make. "Tell them we read their message and we're coming to assist."

"Aye, aye," Boggs said in an overly dramatic manner. He raised the Firefly, which resembled an oversized flashlight, but served as a miniature searchlight.

"Should we notify the Mexican Coast Guard, Captain?" Frank Tell inquired. He was a kid, fresh out of high school. Working as a deck hand on *Neptune's Dream* had been his first real job and he'd pleased Wakely and the others by respecting their seniority and following orders.

"Not unless we have to," the captain answered. "No need to let them know we're out here. I'd prefer to keep that from becoming public information if we can. Of course, if that distressed vessel needs more help than we can give, we'll have to do what's right."

Boggs began flashing out a reply to the other boat's message in Morse code while Wakely returned to the helm and took over the wheel. He changed the heading to 110 degrees and steered *Neptune's Dream* toward the troubled vessel. The blinking light in the fog soon appeared in Wakely's view. It executed a series of quick winking dots and prolonged dashes. The captain's Morse code was a little rusty and he wasn't certain what the message meant. Luckily, Boggs appeared in the wheelhouse with a translation.

"Sir," he began. "They say they want to send an injured man over in a small boat."

Wakely grunted. "What the hell can we do for him? Do they think we've got a doctor on board?"

Boggs relayed a modified version of the captain's testy remarks to the distressed ship. The light flickered in reply. "They say they're be-calmed and the auxilary is down with a burnt valve from tryin' to make harbor against the tide in this fog."

The captain scowled. Damn poor seamanship by his reckoning. "Better drop anchor. Don't want to have a collision with the poor bastard. Tell Al to prepare to receive company."

"Aye, aye, Captain," Boggs replied in a serious tone, which was his form of sarcasm. Wakely and the rest of the crew never realized this.

Wakely throttled back the engine and left the helm to return to the deck. The anchor chain rattled noisily out through the hawsehole. In the sudden silence, small wavelets slapped noisily against the lapstrake sides of *Neptune's Dream's* hull. The blinking light had stopped. The deck canted while a long swell caused the trawler to roll and drifted the outline of a long, white sailboat into visibility in the thick mist. Judging from what he could see in the fog, Wakely reckoned she was a thirty-nine foot ketch-rigged schooner. He snorted with distaste, having nothing but contempt for amateurs who treated boats as playthings. The sea demanded respect and it was a place for working men, not loafers.

Odd. Although the captain realized what the schooner must be, he still felt a tremble of fear slither along his backbone. The pale shape in the fog resembled a ghost ship. Tales of the *Flying Dutchman* rushed into Wakely's mind.

Then the sound of a small outboard motor reached his ears. Wakely chided himself for allowing superstitions—another old tradition of men of the sea—to cause such illogical notions.

After all, ghosts don't need motorboats. Still, he couldn't shake his apprehension. A man like Solomon Wakely always listened to his intincts and they were screaming at him that something was terribly wrong indeed.

The brilliant glare of an ACR-L6A Super Beam "gun" knifed through the mist, drawing closer to *Neptune's Dream* while the sputter of the outboard increased. The bright circlet of light in the fog reminded Wakely of the stories about mysterious "foo fighters" that supposedly harassed pilots in World War II. More nonsense, he told himself. He'd seen nothing like that on the North Atlantic run. He glanced back into the dense fog to study the oncoming craft. Nothing seemed sinister about the skiff however the occupants were a different matter.

The man at the tiller was a wiry, ferret-faced individual with a neatly trimmed beard, laced with streaks of gray. He wore a U.S. Navy deck jacket and a black wool cap. Although he did not appear to be more than forty years old, wrinkles surrounded his eyes when he smiled up at Wakely's crew. The captain immediately disliked the man. He looked like a professional politician who'd fallen on hard times.

The boat came to a halt alongside *Neptune's Dream*. Two other men slowly rose from the narrow benches amidships of the tiny vessel. They were a classical Mutt and Jeff pair—although nothing about them amused Wakely. The smaller of the two was painfully thin with a corpse-like complexion and such deep-set eyes the sockets seemed to be empty in the dim light.

His companion stood over six feet tall with a barrel chest and wide shoulders that would have done justice to a stevedore. A broad grin decorated his wide face. The smile bothered Wakely. It seemed to possess a cruel, smirking quality. A Charles Manson smile.

"Ahoy there," the pilot of the skiff called to Wakely's crew. "You fellas are angels of mercy at sea."

"Common courtesy, friend," Wakely replied. His men threw lines down to the smaller boat. "You said you have an injured man?"

"That's right," the man answered, watching his two-man crew tie the lines to a pair of rowlocks, which swung it in close alongside *Neptune's Dream*. "Got him on a stretcher here. Appreciate some help getting him aboard."

"Rig out the net boom," Wakely ordered. His crew jumped to obey. The captain frowned. "What's wrong with your man?" He suspected the newcomers might be drug smugglers or gun runners and one of their gang had caught a bullet. He didn't relish welcoming such hoodlums.

"Shark got him," came the reply. "Young rich kid named Daniel Woton. Got us to crew his schooner so he could go frolic in the ocean. Idiot decided to take a moonlight swim and damned if a shark didn't come along to play with him."

The Mutt and Jeff team raised a fourth figure from the thwarts of the small boat. The young man was strapped to a stretcher, his body covered by two thick wool blankets. Only a slight movement of his blond-haired head suggested that he was still alive.

"Have you radioed for help?" Wakely inquired over the loud rattle of cable when the hoist capstan ran out the boom. The visitors hauled on the free end of the device and quickly rigged a sling under the stretcher. The Jeff type gave a thumbs up signal and the net boom took the strain.

"Radio's out," the skipper announced as he climbed up the side. The injured party cleared the weather rail of *Neptune's Dream* and Boggs and Tell pulled the stretcher on board. "Silly bastard didn't ever pull maintenance on his fancy rig," he continued, "So, no radio, first aid kit, flares, nothing."

"Since you seem to be in charge of the crew shouldn't you have seen to the equipment, Mister . . . ?"

"Linsey," he replied, offering his hand. "Joe Linsey."

Wakely took his hand. Linsey pumped the captain's arm three times, shaking hands like a politician.

"Yeah," he admitted. "I suppose I should have figured the kid would fuck up. Should have taken more care in checking things out before we left for Baja."

"We can take this fellah down to our cabin," Frank Tell offered. He and Boggs bunked together and he was youthfully eager to help an injured person.

"All right," Wakely agreed. "But I want Jim to radio the Mexicans immediately."

"Jake," Linsey told the scrawny cadaverous man. "Help take Woton down to this young fellah's cabin." He turned to the larger member of his crew. "Wait here, Bruno."

"Right, Joe," the little man answered. His brutish companion merely nodded in response.

"Bet you gents could use some hot coffee with a little rum in it," Al Fontaine remarked with a nervous smile. He didn't like the looks of the three strangers, but they could hardly throw the trio overboard for that.

"That's to my taste," Linsey admitted. "But Woton needs some attention. That shark took a chunk out of his leg and all we could do was improvise some bandages and a tourniquet."

"I've got some first aid gear on the bridge," Wakely stated.

"That's fine, Captain," Linsey said, displaying his oily politician's smile.

Frank and Jake awkwardly carried Woton across the deck to the boy's cabin. Fontaine hurried off to prepare some rum-spiked coffee while Wakely and Boggs headed for the helm, followed by Linsey. Bruno, the big man with the snide smile, seemed content to merely stand on the deck and grin at the others as though waiting for a bizarre practical joke to take place.

A locker built into the back wall of the wheelhouse of *Neptune's Dream* contained most of the boat's vital equipment, including navigational gear, the radio and a well-stocked medical supply cabinet. Boggs quickly stationed himself at the radio, while the captain marched to the cabinet. Linsey leaned against the door frame and watched them, calmly unbuttoning his jacket.

"Is Woton in shock?" Wakely inquired, rummaging through his medical supplies.

"Probably," Linsey replied with a shrug.

"What's the name of your boat, Mr. Linsey?" Boggs asked, picking up the radio microphone. "I'll need it to call in a Mayday to the Mexican Coast Guard."

"But this isn't a Mayday," Linsey smiled as he inserted a hand inside his jacket. "It's a Doomsday—for *you!*"

Then he drew a Walther P-38 and aimed it at the startled young man's face. Jim Boggs' mouth fell open in astonishment a split second before Linsey squeezed the trigger.

The pistol cracked sharply and a round-nosed nine-millimeter projectile drilled a ragged hole between Boggs' terrified eyes. The bullet tunneled through his brain and popped the back of Boggs' skull open to splatter gore across the radio set.

Captain Wakely whirled to face Linsey. His muscles froze with fear and confusion. Why was this happening? What could he do? How would God judge him in the next world? Armed only with a box of bandages and a bottle of antiseptic liquid, Wakely stared at the gun in Linsey's hand and waited for the next shot which would signal his death.

"Give my regards to Davey Jones," Linsey chuckled.

He fired two rounds into Wakely's chest. The 9mm slugs kicked the captain back into the locker. Burning agony filled Wakely's torso and formed an iron vice around his lungs. He tried to think. Damn it! When a man is about to die, he should think of *something*! Then his heart ceased to function and consciousness fled as the captain fell face-first to the deck.

Frank Tell and Jake had placed Woton on the boy's bunk and loosened the straps to the stretcher when they heard the pistol shots. Frank flinched, his entire body recoiling from the sound.

"What was that?" he wondered aloud, fearfully glancing at Jake.

The emaciated sailor's face remained devoid of expression. He slowly drew a snubnosed revolver from the pocket of his Navy peacoat.

"No!" Frank shouted, lunging forward in sheer desperation and frightened reflex.

He caught Jake off guard and literally shoved him into the air with both hands. Inept though the boy's response had been, it still sent the scrawny gunman hurtling across the room. Jake's elbow struck the corner of a heavy sea chest, jarring the ulna nerve. His revolver popped out of numb fingers and fell to the floor.

Frank stared down at the gun and then bent to reach for it. A tremendous roar filled the small cabin and a tidal wave of lead pellets pulverized Frank's chest and face. The blast pitched his body backward to tumble through the open hatchway. His corpse fell in a ragged heap across the threshold.

Daniel Woton sat up on the bunk, the blankets bunched together at his legs. Smoke curled from the muzzle of the sawed-off, 10 gauge, double-barreled shotgun in his hands.

Al Fontaine's response to the gunshots had been typical of his slow mind. When he'd heard the report of Linsey's pistol, Al abandoned the coffee pot and rum bottle in the tiny galley of *Neptune's Dream* and stared at the door, half expecting someone to rush in and either tell him what had happened or shoot him down. The bellow of the shotgun convinced him to take some sort of action.

"Better ask the captain," he decided aloud, desperately hoping Wakely would be in a condition that would allow him to give advice.

Al stepped onto the deck and headed toward the helm on rubber legs. He turned the corner of the cabin section to encounter a formidable dark hulk in the fog. The figure stepped closer. Al stared up at Bruno's cruel, grinning face.

Fontaine wasn't exactly a ninety-five pound weakling himself. He reacted to the threat in a manner that suited a veteran of a hundred brawls in harbor taverns. Al swung a hard right cross at Bruno's face. Knuckles connected with jawbone and Al felt the satisfying vibration of the impact of his punch travel through his arm to his shoulder.

Bruno's head barely jerked to the side from the blow and the crazy smile remained fixed on his ugly face.

Before the startled Fontaine could make another move, Bruno struck. A big fist rammed into Al's midsection with sledgehammer force. Fontaine gasped and doubled up, feeling as if his stomach had been ruptured and wrapped around his backbone. Bruno uttered a deep, cold laugh and seized Al's head, grabbing his hair with one hand and gripping his jaw with the other. The brute's great shoulders revolved sharply as he viciously twisted Fontaine's head. Neck vertebrae cracked loudly. Bruno released his victim. Al fell heavily to the deck. Although he lay on his belly, Fontaine's lifeless eyes stared up at the fog-covered sky.

Joe Linsey emerged from the wheelhouse, his Walther P-39 held ready. He approached Bruno and stared down at the corpse that had formerly been Al Fontaine. Linsey effectively concealed his revulsion for Bruno's methods. Christ, if the guy had done the special effects in *The Exorcist*, Linda Blair never would have made another movie!

"Nice work, Bruno," Linsey remarked, afraid to say anything else.

The behemoth nodded with satisfaction.

Jake and Woton strolled toward the pair, the latter carrying his shotgun canted over a shoulder. "You got the kid?" Linsey inquired.

"No thanks to Jake," Woton replied dryly. "He fumbled the ball, but me and my cannon saved the day."

Jake sniveled and shrugged helplessly.

"What matters is we took care of all of them," Linsey stated, returning his pistol to its shoulder holster under his peacoat. "Congratulations, fellahs. We got ourselves another boat."

"Ain't much of one if'n you ask me," Jake muttered.

"Nobody asked you, fuckhead," Linsey replied sharply. "Sure, this old tub isn't exactly the Queen Mary, but we've got a deadline to meet. This rig will come in useful. Believe me."

"I still wish I knew what the hell the boss was planning to do with these things," Woton commented, breaking open his shotgun to remove the spent shell casing.

"When the time comes for you to know, we'll

tell you," Linsey assured him, avoiding the fact that he was not entirely aware of the purpose himself. "Besides, if I told you about it now, you'd never believe it." He abruptly changed subjects, his voice crackling with command. "Get that anchor up and let's haul ass. It's a long way to Cabo San Lucas and a lot further to where we're going."

2

Taking It Easy

Mark Hardin strolled along the pier at Newport
Beach and wistfully examined the rows of beautiful blue water boats docked in the harbor.
They seemed to be ships of a fantasy world,
polished ivory vessels for Ulysses, Sinbad, or
Jason and the Argonauts to sail off on magical
adventures in exotic lands. Deceptively frail in
appearance, in the right hands they were sturdy
enough to survive anything short of a hurricane.
Even anchored in the marina, they had a quality of grace and dignity, eager to sail into a
dimension of dreams . . .

Dreams, Mark thought, forcing his mind back
to reality. To the man known throughout the
world as the *Penetrator*, reality consisted of fighting criminal syndicates, insidious conspiracies
and inconceivable danger. He ought to be shop-
ping for a cemetery plot instead of a pleasure
craft.

Mark didn't appear to be a man who'd be
contemplating his own death. Still in his early
thirties, he was six foot two and athletically fit,
with broad shoulders, powerful limbs, a solid
strong chest and a lean waist. True, he could

present a formidable appearance. Mark's dark, aristocratic features revealed his half-Cheyenne ancestry and took on a deadly aura when he frowned.

This might give *others* cause to fear for their lives—and often the feeling proved accurate. Yet, a young man in superb physical condition had no business thinking about coffins and grave-yards while surrounded by the magnificent Pacific Ocean, a clear blue sky and a fleet of majestic white yachts. Especially since he could easily afford one of the boats—unless that young man happened to be the Penetrator.

Many people who'd followed the adventures of this incredible crime fighter and fabled one-man army, tended to think of the Penetrator as impervious to harm and immune to death. Mark Hardin knew better. He'd been shot, stabbed, cut and slugged enough times to appreciate his own mortality.

True, a warrior acquires more expertise and greater ability through experience, yet his odds of encountering a lethal bullet wound or knife thrust increased with time. Few, if any, warriors had ever survived as many battlefields in numerous different situations, against various types of opponents as the Penetrator.

His first battleground had been one many young men could relate to: Vietnam. As an intelligence sergeant in the Special Operations Group, MAC V, Mark saw plenty of action in the jungles of Southeast Asia, which included bold probes behind enemy lines. On two occasions, he went into the heart of North Vietnam to terminate high-ranking NVA officers and Communist civilian leaders.

Yet, during his second tour to 'Nam, he discovered an enemy within the U.S. Army itself. He learned of a large black market ring in Saigon, involving numerous American military personnel, a brigadier general among them. After Mark reported his evidence, no arrests followed, so he took his story to the AP wire service in Saigon. Soon, the information became international news and the military quickly took the guilty into custody. At least, most of them.

Several black marketeers who'd escaped the Army's dragnet lured Mark into an abandoned warehouse and attempted to beat him to death. They nearly succeeded. His body required long months before it finally healed and Mark was given an honorable discharge for medical reasons. He left the military, a disenchanted and bitter young man.

However, Mark's former football coach from UCLA suggested a treatment the doctors never thought of. At his advice, Mark traveled to the Calico Mountains in California's Mojave Desert and met Professor Willard Haskins. They formed an immediate friendship and Mark agreed to stay at Haskins' fabulous underground mansion, which even then he called the Stronghold.

From that point, events and Fate began to transform Mark Hardin's life forever. A wandering Cheyenne medicine chief, David Red Eagle, came upon the scene and immediately recognized Mark as one of "the Beautiful People." Indeed, an investigation into Mark's past discovered that he was half Cheyenne Indian. David undertook the task of restoring his self-claimed protege's physical and emotional health and succeeded to a remarkable, almost supernatural degree. Mark was soon stronger and more fit than before he'd suffered the beating in Saigon, and his senses and reflexes had been conditioned to a level even jungle combat hadn't developed.

Then Donna Morgan, Haskins' beautiful and noble niece, came into Mark's life. The couple fell in love and their future seemed full of promise . . . until Fate spat on their happiness. Donna fell victim to the Mafia family of Don Pietro Scarelli and Mark Hardin struck back with a vengeance, using the combined lethal abilities of his military training and Vietnam combat experience and the skills of a Cheyenne Dog Soldier to crush the mob in a bloody one-man war.

Thus, the Penetrator was created—conceived in the violence of Southeast Asia, born amid the love and well-meaning of the Stronghold and baptized in the fire of revenge.

The Scarelli incident proved to be the first of many missions for Mark Hardin. Since then, the Penetrator had faced every conceivable type of adversary: from crooked killer cops in Seattle to the Aryan Brotherhood in Salt Lake City. He'd hunted down white collar criminals and gun-wielding terrorists. The Mafia, the KGB, Nazis in Brazil and international conspirators had all felt his fearsome wrath.

Since Mark had become the Penetrator, a name given him by the sensation-hungry press, he'd successfully accomplished fifty such missions. How much longer could his luck hold out? No man, no matter how well trained, experienced or armed with the best weapons available for the task, could expect to survive many more operations that contained immeasurable risk to life and limb.

Yet, from the beginning Mark had accepted the fact that violent death would one day claim him. He'd been startled to live past thirty and was certain he'd never see his fortieth birthday. Until recently, this hadn't seemed too important to the fiercely dedicated warrior known as the Penetrator.

He'd known many women over the years and genuinely loved some of them. Yet, even the lovely and courageous Joanna Tabler, who'd shared numerous adventures with Mark before she, too, became a victim in the endless war with Evil, could not replace the part of his heart that had perished with Donna Morgan. He had been certain he could never love anyone so completely again and any hope for a wife and family had been lost with Donna all those long, empty years ago.

Then Mark met Angie Dillon and he hadn't been quite the same since.

The Penetrator had made a conscious effort to push Angie from his thoughts and heart, fearing for her safety and the well-being of her delightful children, Kevin and Karen. He also secretly feared that he'd once again lose what he loved most in the world. Mark didn't know if he could endure that emotional agony once more. He'd rather take a bullet in the heart than have it broken a second time.

Even the Penetrator's constant war with the Dark Forces throughout the world left him some time for a rather fragmented personal life. Despite his better judgement, Mark's longing to be with Angie and the kids drew him to them time and again. Not long ago, the children had nearly become victims of a grotesque scheme of the SIE, a conspiracy of One-World elitists. Mark vowed that they'd never be placed in danger due to one of his missions again. Yet, how could he be certain he would be able to keep that promise so long as he continued to be the Penetrator?

Christ, how much is one man supposed to do? Mark thought bitterly. Why couldn't someone else slay the dragons once in a while? He'd done more than his share. Didn't he deserve to be free of the hellfire and brimstone of combat and death? If he had no time for a life of his own, he admonished himself, he had even less for self-pity.

A rare smile crept across Mark's face when he once again stared at the yachts and allowed his imagination to wander.

A good forty-two footer could take them away from all the madness that filled his life as the Penetrator. They could take a two year cruise around the world. Why not? Mark had more than ample funds stored away to live comfortably for the rest of his life—and to support a family of one beautiful, wonderful wife and two terrific children. A couple more kids, for all of that. Angie would love such a voyage and what better education could the twins have than to actually visit other countries and travel the entire globe?

It's not merely a daydream, he told himself, gazing at the rippling green-blue ocean that met the lavender horizon laced with white clouds and populated by gliding sea gulls. If the Penetrator disappeared for two years or so, the various criminal organizations and espionage agencies that stalked him—to say nothing of the FBI and other law enforcement outfits who tended to regard him as an outlaw—would assume their quarry had died. It wasn't too late for Mark Hardin to have a family and a peaceful life of love and sanity—was it?

"Beautiful, aren't they?" a masculine voice inquired behind Mark. The inflection indicated more than normal curiosity by the question.

Mark glanced over his shoulder to see a large, beefy man dressed in pressed khaki shorts and a matching shirt. Something seemed familiar about the broad face, good-natured smile and unruly shock of dark blond hair that hung over the fellow's forehead. No danger signals flashed inside his head, so the Penetrator smiled in return.

"You mean the boats?" he offered.

" 'Course I do," the man replied. "See something you like? You know, you can lease one of those beauties for the weekend for a lot less than you probably imagine. Can also buy on the installment plan if you're interested, or finance it through your bank. 'Course, you'll probably want'a take one out in the bay first ..." An appealing salesman's smile blossomed.

"Well," Mark began slowly, trying to keep his tongue from responding too quickly. "I might be interested later ..."

"Sounds like you're interested right now, but you ..." the salesman's pitch stopped abruptly and his brow crinkled while he stared at the Penetrator as though seeing him for the first time.

"Hot damnation on a chocolate sundae!" he exclaimed. "It's Mark Hardin, for Crisssake!"

The Penetrator searched the other man's face,

trying to mentally picture it younger, without the beginning of a double chin beneath the jaw.

"Clell?" he asked, uncertain, "Clell Brockman?"

"You got it," the salesman declared, taking Mark's hand and shaking it vigorously. "Man, UCLA was a long time ago."

"A lifetime ago," Mark agreed.

"The good old days, huh?" Brockman sighed. "Things were sure different then. Including me," he patted the bulge at his stomach, the beginnings of a pot belly. "No team would have me for a reserve quarterback these days."

Then Brockman scanned over the Penetrator's trim physique, clad in white duck slacks and a cream-colored T-shirt. "You sure managed to stay in shape. How'd you do it?"

"Well, I ..." Mark began, trying to think of how to cope with the avalanche of questions that were bound to follow.

"You in professional sports?" Brockman asked. "I played pro ball with the Chargers for a season when I first got outta college. Halfback. That's when I started to put on weight. 'Course, they had me on the bench most of the time. We played Dallas once and they put me in the game for a change, right? Well, these two guys built like Texas tanks ran over my ass and broke my leg in two places. About as bad as what happened to you that one time back in college. Remember when those guys hit you like a ton of concrete muscle?"

"Oh, yeah," Mark nodded.

"Aw, hell," Clell moaned. "That was a dumb thing to say. Those bastards almost broke your back. Hey, let me buy you a drink and we can talk in a more relaxed atmosphere."

Soon they were seated at a bar in the Poseidon Lounge. The two men sipped piña coladas. Mark glanced about the quiet little tavern which had been decorated with starfish and maritime paintings on the walls, with chandeliers that consisted of imitation ship's wheels with electrical lamps attached. He had forgotten that Clell could be a first class motormouth—a trait which the Penetrator blessed under the circumstances because it gave him time to think of a cover story.

"Hey, you went into the army, didn't you?" Brockman remarked, fishing a pack of Camel Lights from a shirt pocket. "Yeah. None of the old gang ever heard from you after that. We sorta figured you got killed in 'Nam or something."

"Not quite," Mark said dryly.

"What you been doing since the war?" Brockman pressed, lighting a cigarette.

"Well . . ." the Penetrator hadn't quite decided what to tell the guy.

Clell's verbal trots again came to Mark's rescue. "Know what I got into? I'm a yacht broker now. Yeah. Those blue water babies out there are my bread and butter. Make a nice living at it too. Hey, didn't you used to do a lot of sailing back when you were dating what's-her-name?"

"Sylvia Carpenter," Mark recalled his old girlfriend. "Her father was the vice president of Laslo Plastics and he gave Sylvia a yacht on her eighteenth birthday. We spent a lot of time on the boat before we went our separate ways."

"Still remember how to handle a boat like that?" Brockman inquired.

"Sure," the Penetrator replied. "In fact, I've been thinking about getting one . . ."

"Great," Clell interrupted, assuming the sale in approved fashion, pointing at Mark with the tip of his cigarette. "How'd you like a chance to try your hand at it again before you make up your mind one way or the other?"

"You have something in mind?" Mark asked, helping himself to a bowl of roasted peanuts on the bar.

"I've got this lovely little Newport ketch," Brockman began, stabbing out his smoke in an ashtray. "The *All American*. Sold it to an old football chum. One of those Dallas tanks that busted my leg, believe it or not. Anyway, I have to take it through the Canal and deliver it to the guy in shit-stomper land. Already hired a kid named Dennis something-or-other, but he's young and inexperienced. He can handle the scut work, but what I really need is a genuine blue water sailor like you to crew for me."

Mark could hardly believe such an opportunity had suddenly fallen into his lap. "T—that sounds great, Clell . . ."

"But if you can't get away for a few days," Brockman shrugged. "What did you say you do for a living?"

Mark was ready for him now. "I'm an international courier. I've been working out of U.S. embassies all over the world for the last ten years. South America, Europe, Japan, all those places."

"No kidding?" Brockman's eyes widened. "Man, I bet you've got some stories to tell."

"A couple." The Penetrator congratulated himself on the cover he'd conjured up. It would allow him to talk about foreign lands he'd visited without making Clell suspicious. After all, he'd probably get a chance to say *something* if they were going to be sailing to Texas from California together.

3

Sharks In Paradise

"Nuts," Clell Brockman muttered. "This gale is gonna blow us off course."

The problem wasn't really serious, but it had been the closest thing to a disturbance that had occurred since the *All American* left Newport Beach and headed down the West Coast to Cabo San Lucas at the tip of Baja. Mark Hardin quickly headed toward the stern of the boat, and grabbed the backstays.

"Better shorten the canvas," he announced. "Dennis, you get the shrouds and adjust them in the deadeyes. I'll take care of the mainsheets."

"Aye, aye," Dennis Richards replied dully, shuffling over to the lines that extended from the masthead to the bulwarks of the vessel.

Mark glanced at the slender, long-haired youth dressed in the same ragged denim cut-offs and soiled T-shirt he'd worn since the trip began. The Penetrator could think of better company for the cruise than a rather lazy, slightly insolent kid, but renewing his friendship with Clell Brockman had been pleasant enough and the trip along the coast of Baja served as a mini-version of his dream retirement—which appealed to him more with each passing day.

Mark and Dennis slowly lowered the lifts and yards of the mast to shorten the sail while Brockman handled the wheel to keep them on course. In the gale the auto-pilot would be useless. The crisis, if one happened to be melodramatic enough to call it one, was over. Clell descended into the cabin when Mark took the wheel, and returned with three cold cans of Tecate beer from the ice chest on the spar deck.

"So far, so good, gents," he declared, handing Mark and Dennis each a brew.

"Thanks, Clell," Mark said, taking his beer.

"Hope we come across some more boats," Dennis stated, slurping his Tecate. " 'Specially if they've got a bunch of pussy sunning on deck in bikinis, like we seen yesterday."

"You're a real class act, kid," Brockman muttered. "How about checking those lanyards before you go to your cuddy and play with yourself? The ones over there on the poop?"

"Figures," Dennis snickered. "I get all the shitty jobs." He chuckled at his own joke as he headed for the tack rail.

"Cute," Clell rolled his eyes. Then he turned to Mark. "Well, how are you enjoying the trip so far?"

"Terrific," the Penetrator replied, staring at the countless miles of ocean and sky that surrounded their graceful white craft. A gentle, rolling swell lifted the bow and sweetly kissed the stern with an easy, rocking chair motion. Flying fish broke the surface at the bowsprit and a pair of dolphins chased each other along the gleaming strakes and under the keel. Mark noticed several large black lumps rolling along the waves at about ten knots.

Clell smiled and reached for a pair of 7 × 50 binoculars. "School of blackfish," he explained, raising the field glasses to his eyes.

"Blackfish?" Mark inquired.

"Dumb name for 'em, really," Brockman remarked, handing the glasses to the Penetrator. "They're actually whales. First cousin of the Orca, but better natured."

Mark saw the school clearly through the binoculars. The great black sea mammals indeed resembled the trained killer whales he'd seen at Sea World in San Diego, except they lacked the Orca's white coloring at the belly and their snouts were rounder. The Penetrator counted nine adults in the school and four calves.

"You see a lot of blackfish around here," Brockman stated, digging his cigarettes out of a pocket. "No Japs or Russkies to kill 'em off. Everything seems to be at peace with nature out here and . . ." Clell broke off and smiled. "Shit, I sound like an ecology freak, but it's true. When I get ready to retire, I'm gonna get Betty on one of these rigs that'll be our very own property and we'll only go back to shore to pick up beer and steaks."

"Not a bad idea," Mark observed softly, envying the whales and Brockman. Yet, why couldn't he do the same? He, Angie and the kids with a two year supply of traveler's checks and two thirds of the world to sail on. Why the hell not?

Dinner consisted of beef stew cooked on a butane stove in the galley and, naturally, another round of beer. The trio ate on the deck at dusk. The offshore breeze had begun and bent their course further from land, yet the rich earth scent and pungent aroma of desert vegetation came clearly to them. As it happens at sea, the sun seemed to rapidly plunge toward the undulating breast of the ocean. Great long rollers appeared to devour crescent bites of the red-orange ball, promising a spectacular sunset. Mark and Clell sat wordlessly, transfixed by the splendor.

Even Dennis remained silent while they watched the spectacle of sundown on the sea. The fiery orb developed an almost tender shade of orange, laced with a rainbow of other colors: pink, yellow, purple. Shards of light seemed to slide across the waves when the sun began to sink below the horizon. In the last, lingering moment, the trio witnessed a rare but vivid flash of emerald green. Yeah, the Penetrator thought, when I get back to the States, Angie and I have got to have a talk.

"Good omen, or bad?" Clell asked in an awed voice.

"What?" Mark came back, his reverie broken.

"The green flash. You know what they say."

"I don't know. We'll just have to wait and see."

From Cabo San Lucas, the *All American* cut diagonally southeast to Acapulco and then turned due south toward the Guatamalan coastline. On the seventh day of their cruise, the boat sailed in calm, gentle waters, seemingly all alone in the Pacific. Then, shortly after noon, they encountered another vessel, a fishing trawler flying the American flag.

"Ahoy, the boat!" an amplified voice called to

them, boosted by a megaphone. The ocean helped carry the sound, but broke up the meaning. "We need assistance! Can you help?"

Clell opened a compartment built into the transom behind the wheel. It contained several items of emergency gear, including a megaphone, ACR/4F Firefly signal light and a 25mm Mayday flare pistol. He picked up the megaphone to reply to the distress call.

"Ahoy, trawler!" Brockman's amplified voice echoed across the ocean. "Stand by, we'll come alongside."

Mark hefted Brockman's binoculars and trained them on the fishing boat. The legend *Sea Serpent* had been painted on the bow and across the stern. To the Penetrator's trained eye, the names seemed unaccountably fresh and he thought he saw the smudged letters of another name beneath, N-E-P-T-U, hastily and imperfectly covered over. While the vessels drew nearer, he spotted a figure holding a megaphone, probably the skipper of the trawler.

"Negative. Request you receive a small boat. We need to use your radio to contact the Guatamalan Maritime authorities," the man called to the *All American*. "Ours is out of order." The two craft were less than twenty yards apart, making conversation easier.

"Should have paid your bill to Ma Bell," Brockman joked through the megaphone. "We'll be happy to receive your party."

Mark watched the skipper of the *Sea Serpent* lower his bullhorn. A sly smile crept across the man's fox-like, bearded face and a cold shiver slid along the Penetrator's spine. He thought of the painted-out name. Neptune something or other. Within seconds, a small net-tending dory, equipped with an outboard motor, cut across the water toward the *All American*. Four men were inside the tiny craft.

"They must have had the boat ready before they called to us," Mark observed, suspicion in his tone.

"Yeah," Brockman shrugged. "Must not want to waste any time. Wonder what's wrong?"

"Probably figured we'd help 'em," Dennis added, inanely fondling a large steel wrench.

"Uh-huh," Mark grunted. "And they're sending *four* guys to use the radio?"

"Jesus, Mark," Brockman sighed. "You must have gotten paranoid after all that international intrigue stuff when you were a courier. Don't get up tight."

The Penetrator realized his friend might have a point. After years of dealing with super criminals and their insidious plots, he could be jumping to conclusions, seeing danger in an odd, yet innocent, action by the crew of the *Sea Serpent*. Still, he'd also developed a sixth sense for combat, a survival instinct that signaled danger. It was sending an alarm to his brain when the dory approached the starboard side.

Although Mark hadn't expected trouble when he'd agreed to sail with Brockman, he could never forget he was the Penetrator. He'd brought a .45 caliber Star PD and a couple of golf-ball sized WP grenades just in case one of his numerous enemies managed to track him down. It had happened before.

However, this didn't seem likely to occur on a quiet cruise along the coast of Mexico, so Mark had left his pistol and grenades locked in an attaché case in his cuddy. The only weapon Mark carried on his person during the trip was a Guardfather—a handy little item that appeared to be an innocent black metal pen—in his shirt pocket. He mentally debated going to his cabin for the other weapons, but the skiff had already pulled alongside the *All American*.

"Sure glad you fellas agreed to help us out," Jake Leiter remarked, tossing a rope up to Dennis. The kid eagerly caught it and tied the line to a halyard cleat.

"Yeah," Daniel Woton added as he climbed over the rail of the *All American*. He carried a bulky canvas sack slung over his shoulder. "Mighty hospitable of you."

The Penetrator's combat instinct rattled a warning inside his head when he saw Woton's bundle. It contained an object, thick at one end and narrow at the other, which to Mark looked suspiciously like it could be a sawed-off shotgun or rifle with a cut-down stock. The other three wore jackets—in 80 degree subtropical weather?

"Paranoid, hell," Mark muttered when he saw the familiar bulge under the left armpit of one of the men. The guy was packing a gun and Mark suspected the others were armed as well. Two of them positioned themselves between the Penetrator and the gangway to the cabins, blocking his path to reclaiming his .45.

"I'll show you where the radio is . . ." Brockman began, still blissfully unaware anything was wrong.

"Oh," Jake coldly announced through a wicked smile, drawing his snubnosed .38 from a pocket. "We'll find it!"

Josie Waldo, the man closest to the Penetrator,

noticed a blur of movement when Mark made his move. The thug pulled a .357 Colt Trooper from a shoulder holster under his jacket, but Mark had already closed the distance.

One hand seized Josie's wrist behind the Magnum before he could use it, while the other plucked the Guardfather from its pocket. Mark pressed the clip on the metal "pen" and a solid, ice-pick type blade shot out and locked in place.

Josie caught a glimpse of the instrument in Mark's fist and cried out in terror. The Penetrator's arm flashed and he drove the point of the Guardfather into the hollow of his opponent's throat. Sharp steel punctured Josie's windpipe and trachea and silenced his scream forever.

"Shit!" Woton exclaimed as he unsheathed his 10 gauge shotgun from its sack.

The three surviving hoods—Woton, Jake and Carter—hesitated because Mark still held Josie Waldo in the line of fire. They were unaware the man was already dead. Without warning, the Penetrator shoved Josie's corpse at the trio. Woton and Carter stepped out of its path, but the flabby body crashed into Jake, knocking him over.

Woton had jumped to the bulwark and leaned against the rail when he began to swing his 10 gauge toward Mark. His eyes expanded with fear when he saw the Penetrator, crouched on one knee, both hands fisted around the butt of Josie's .357 Colt. The Magnum roared and a 158 grain hollow point projectile smashed into the center of Daniel Woton's forehead.

The high velocity bullet knifed through the young hood's brain and blew out the top of his head. Woton's body pivoted against the taffrail, nearly falling overboard. His shotgun pointed over the side and a finger, powered by a muscle convulsion, pulled a trigger. The .10 gauge double-bellowed, smashing a handful of .00 buckshot through the bottom of the pirate dory, while the recoil served to kick Woton's faceless corpse backward to fall heavily on the polished teak deck.

Suddenly Brockman bellowed in rage and charged the disoriented Bradley Carter. The gunman lowered the muzzle of his Colt .38 Super and squeezed the trigger. Brockman's howl became one of pain when the bullet drilled into his thigh. He crashed to the teakwood deck, moaning and clawing at his wounded leg.

Before Carter could train his pistol on the Penetrator, the .357 Magnum boomed again. Bradley Carter's body leaped into the air from the force of the slug that struck him in the upper chest. His arms whirled overhead, the .38 Super flying from his grasp. Carter's body fell against the wall of the cabin and slumped to the deck. A large scarlet stain began to form at the front of his jacket.

Where's the fourth one? Mark thought as he slowly rose, the .357 held ready.

Then something connected with the back of his skull. It felt as though he'd been hit by a falling building and the white pain robbed him of vision and turned his muscles into unresponsive mush.

I think I found him ... the Penetrator's mind told him with bitter irony before a black veil descended upon it.

4

Drifting to Hell

The team had won a big game that night. Yeah. They'd beaten Oklahoma U., 16 to 10. Great game. They were entitled to a big party after that. Ned Pierson brought five kegs of beer from his old man's brewery and before long, Mark Hardin was in a chug-a-lug contest with Clell Brockman and Bull Coners. Clell didn't last past the fifth round, but Mark and Bull were still putting the brew down in great, gulping swallows.

Suddenly the beer tasted awful, alkaline and salty, like desert water on tap. Mark began to choke and his stomach threatened to erupt. His nostrils filled with the briny liquid and he started to suffocate in the stuff. Jesus, Bull, you win . . . !

The Penetrator opened his eyes and felt the sting of salt water on the vulnerable orbs. His body floated, face down, and nausea combined with the throbbing pain in his head to cause confusion and disorientation for a few seconds. Then he realized he must be drowning. Mark fought panic and slowly paddled with arms and legs to get his head above water.

Coughing violently, he spat out globs of salt

water and vomit. A great white blur moved in the distance. Mark blinked his brine-galled eyes until his vision cleared to see the *All American* cutting across the waves to join the fishing trawler. The sight served to jar Mark's mind back to reality and the memories of recent events returned with stark clarity.

"Bastards ..." he rasped, his throat still choked with seawater. He watched the two vessels cruise into the distance together and wondered if he'd ever get an opportunity to settle scores with the pirates.

"Mark ..." a voice weakly called out from behind him.

Paddling in the water, the Penetrator turned to see Clell Brockman clinging to the edge of the fishing boat's dory. The tiny craft floated with its gunwhales barely above the surface, its interior rapidly filling with water. Mark mentally fought fatigue and pain and forced his lead-draped limbs to move. After what seemed to be half a mile through quicksand, he swam to the severely damaged skiff.

"I ... thought you ... were dead ..." Brockman gasped, still holding onto the craft's tenuous support.

"We've both got a lot of life left in us, Clell," Mark replied.

He managed to haul himself into the skiff without capsizing it. The water inside the boat was deeper than Mark had feared, though not enough to scuttle them—at least not yet. The thug's shotgun had ripped a gaping hole in the bottom, blasting away part of the keel. Almost an antique, Mark quickly discovered, the dory had been built before the requirement for styrofoam flotation cells. The pirates must have considered it doomed to a quick sinking and abandoned it. Under the circumstances, it had turned out to be a bit of luck for Mark and Clell.

Mark helped Brockman climb into the leaky vessel. More water bubbled up through the buckshot hole. "Try not to move around too much, Clell," Mark advised his friend.

"Don't worry about that," Brockman replied with a mirthless laugh. More water swirled into their doubtful craft.

Suddenly Mark remembered Clell had been shot. He glanced down at the other man's leg. The trousers leg at Brockman's left thigh was stained with blood. To the Penetrator's relief he found a large metal bucket sitting in a corner near the stern. Mark jammed it into the hole in the hull.

"Push down on this and try to plug the leak long enough for me to make a tourniquet," he told Brockman.

"Think it will do any good?" Clell asked, but he obeyed Mark's instructions.

"Shut up with that kind of talk," the Penetrator said in a flat, hard voice. "We're going to be too busy staying alive to waste time thinking about giving up."

In a small, hinge-top metal storage locker, bolted to the stern, he found a monkey wrench, a pair of vice-grips, two sets of needlenose pliers, some bolts, a tube of lube-grease, a handful of heavy marlin hooks and a sixteen-inch screwdriver. Taking the last item, Mark stripped off his shirt and ripped it into shreds.

"What happened after I was slugged?" he inquired, tearing open a rent in Brockman's pants leg. He used part of the shirt for a bandage and twisted another portion into a cord, which he wound around Brockman's thigh above the bullet wound.

"Didn't know you'd been slugged," Clell replied, cold sweat pouring from his brow. "Christ! Never got shot before. Just passed out. Hurts like hell now."

"When it stops hurting is when you should worry," Mark informed him. The Penetrator used the long blade of the screwdriver to tighten the tourniquet. "What happened to Dennis?"

"Don't know for sure," Brockman answered. "I think they killed him."

"You'll have to hold this in place to make certain it's tight enough to stop the bleeding," Mark told him. He tried to keep his face from expressing his concern for Clell. The bullet had struck the inside of Clell's thigh and that could be serious. "At least the seawater will have served as an antiseptic. Shouldn't get an infection."

"It's not too bad, is it?" Brockman inquired. "I mean, I'm only shot in the leg, right?"

"Just hold the tourniquet in place and humor me, okay?" Mark forced a smile. Why tell Brockman that a punctured femoral artery would mean he'd bleed to death in a matter of minutes? Or that the lack of blood seeping from the wound might well mean there was internal bleeding, something Mark couldn't do a damn thing about.

"I've got to do something about this leak." Quickly Mark set to work to patch the leak in a more effective manner. With the monkey wrench and vice-grips he ripped a damaged thwart from the center seat position and measured it against the hole. What could he use to secure it and make the repair watertight?

He recalled the marlin hooks and lube grease. With the two sets of pliers he straightened out the hooks and set half a dozen of them in the wooden seat with the hefty wrench. Then he removed his trousers and smeared them with grease. He jammed them tightly into the gaps around the bucket that protruded through the hull into the sea. Next he clamped the board over all and drove the improvised nails home. Not a professional job, but it would hold . . . for a while. He began to look around for something to use as a bailer.

"Man, no food or water and we're in a leaky fuckin' boat," Brockman snorted. "Some trip I took you on, huh?"

"Unless you planned this to happen, you have no reason to be sorry about it," Mark retorted. "And if you *did*, I'll punch you in the nose."

Brockman laughed weakly. "Okay, but our chances are mighty lousy unless somebody comes along to rescue us, and that doesn't seem very likely out here."

"Things could be worse," the Penetrator replied, bailing out water with a canvas sea anchor he'd located and tied shut at its narrow end. His eyes searched the horizon for any sign of possible rescue.

Then he spotted two large gray-brown dorsal fins slicing through the water, heading straight for the skiff. Judging from the torpedo shapes of the fish, Mark suspected they were tiger sharks, each about eight feet long. Yeah, things could be worse . . .

*   *   *

Kimberly McCulley's pudgy pink fingers danced across the keyboard of the IBM computer console. Names of employees and their salaries appeared in green letters on the gray, irridescent screen. The numerals were instantly added up and the total printed at the bottom. Very well, thought McCulley, punching a record button to file away the information into a memory bank.

Then he typed out the estimation for future expenses. McCulley frowned. The venture would clearly prove to be more costly than he'd first realized, but the proposed profit for the successful execution of their operations and the following profit of future financial endeavors would more than compensate. He typed in the data and waited for the computer to respond.

Abbreviated number-letter combinations appeared on the screen along with the estimated total. McCulley smiled. Yes, it would eventually pay for itself a thousand times over. Everything he'd invested in the project was indeed worthwhile.

"Checked and double checked," he declared, swinging his swivel chair around to face Joe Linsey. "The estimated profit is staggering! Even more than we'd hoped for. Due cause to celebrate, eh, Joseph?"

"Sure," Linsey agreed with a shrug.

He'd sat in the office for twenty minutes while McCulley played with his computer. Linsey knew it was pointless to try to talk to McCulley when he was at the machine and he wasn't even allowed to smoke around the IBM tinker-toy. So he'd waited, wishing he could be somewhere else. Anywhere that he could light up a cigarette.

McCulley waddled across the room to a small

refrigerator in the office. Five foot five and 230 pounds, McCulley was grossly overweight, but he had long ago given up any and all efforts to combat his flabby girth. He opened the fridge and extracted a silver tray filled with small *paté de fois gras* sandwiches, caviar with melba toast wafers and dates coated with sugar.

"Now, let me get the champagne," he declared cheerfully. A gleam appeared in the fat man's clear blue eyes as he carried the tray to a plexi-glass table.

"I'll just have a beer, Kim," Linsey replied.

McCulley clucked his tongue with distaste. Imagine drinking beer with caviar and *paté*! Joseph had much to learn about the finer things in life, McCulley thought. Yet, Linsey had been extremely useful in his role as a pirate commander and McCulley would not have been able to launch his operation without him.

Also, Linsey had a habit of calling McCulley "Kim," an abbreviation he far preferred to his Christian name, *Kimberly*. His parents had wanted a girl so they'd given him that awful feminine name as though to punish him for being born with a penis. McCulley's childhood had consisted of misery and embarrassment. Short, fat and labeled with a girl's name, he had been taunted and tormented throughout his boyhood and learned to dispise his peers.

Yet, he'd always done well in academic pursuits. McCulley had a natural gift for mathematics and he soon learned to use his mental abilities to compensate for his physical flaws. When other boys were playing in Little League and reading comic books, young Kimberly studied the careers of Andrew Carnegie, John D. Rockefeller and J.P. Morgan. Instead of dating girls or going to football games, he pored over the daily stock reports and copies of *The Wall Street Journal*. By the age of twenty he had become a successful stock broker. At eighteen he had taken a small family inheritance and turned it into a personal fortune of 2.5 million dollars and earned a reputation as a boy genius in the field of economics and finance. At twenty-two he had published two books on the subject and opened his first tax-shelter trust bank.

Unfortunately, McCulley's mind had developed a warped criminal trait and a burning desire for power. He'd discovered that a clever white collar manipulator could acquire more money by cunning and skill than any gun-toting bank robber could hope to—and with considerably less risk of being caught.

Some judicious book juggling and forgeries on Wall Street allowed him to steal nearly 3 million from unsuspecting clients. By then computers were coming into the fore. He'd used his knowledge of them and an illegal terminal to tap into a major oil company's stock holdings in a computerized account and transfer them to a personalized account he had established under an assumed name. He quickly sold the stocks and acquired an additional 5 million dollars.

Inevitably, the odds caught up with Kimberly McCulley. When it became apparent that an inordinate number of his clients had suffered from computer theft and stock manipulations, the SEC stepped in. They investigated MuCulley's operation. Although they could not prove that he had done it, or even how or when the deed had been done—and McCulley had his ill-gotten profits carefully hidden in a sheltered bank on Grand Cayman—the Securities and Exchange Commission found enough irregularities in how he conducted business to send Kimberly to a federal prison for two years.

McCulley found jail to be no handicap, particularly the country club in which he had been incarcerated. He continued to run his business through his New York office and used his spare time to study several new areas of finance, earning his degree in economics from a major eastern university. After his release, shortly before he left the United States for Costa Rica, McCulley took several counterfeit account fund withdrawal slips—which had been easily duplicated by a Xerox color copier—to five different branches of the Bank of America and Chase Manhattan and promptly swindled his wealthiest clients of a grand total of 10 million dollars in one day.

That had merely been the start of a scheme he'd planned for years. With his enormous capital he could easily finance a twisted dream that promised to fulfill his ambitions for wealth, influence and power.

"Yes, Joseph," he began, easing the cork from a champagne bottle. "Even as we speak, the colonel is training my mercenary army in Honduras."

"Yeah, I know," Linsey said as he popped the lid of his beer bottle. Hell, he ought to, he'd been there enough times.

McCulley combed back his flowing blond-brown hair with blunt fingers and smiled. "Think of it, Joseph!" he declared, staring into the future in his mind's eye. "When we seize the island of Guadalupe and take it from those incompetant French imbeciles, we'll be able to establish the financial paradise I've planned for so many years.

"A perfect haven for anyone with a great deal of money, who doesn't want it or its source to become public knowledge," McCulley chuckled, pouring champagne into a chilled goblet. "I'll set up special investment banks with numbered accounts that offer total secrecy for clients," McCulley jabbed a thick finger at Linsey. "And I'll see to it that security is upheld—so long as my clients agree to my terms concerning my share, or rather *our* share, of the interest earned by the investments. Everyone will make an astonishing profit. I know the stock market, the gold exchange and how the international banking community operates on loans to foreign countries. If I have access to enough money, we can make billions, Joseph. *Billions*!" He raised his glass and drank deeply in tribute to his genius.

"Potential clients are everywhere," Kimberly went on. "People who've made a pretty penny by embezzlement or selling heroin, cocaine or other drugs, members of the *Cosa Nostra* and the *Union de Corse* who realize Swiss bank accounts are no longer safe from the prying of the U. S. Government and other agencies. That's to say nothing of certain members of the Third Reich in Brazil and Paraguay who don't want their accounts to lead Israeli agents to their current address," McCulley continued. "Of course, we'll also have legalized gambling casinos and prostitution—that will cater to every conceivable taste—all owned and operated by the government. *Our* government.

"And if anyone wants to come to our little kingdom on a more or less permanent basis, he or she will be granted instant citizenship ... providing that person can meet certain financial requirements. Naturally, we'll accept absolutely no extradition agreements with any government, thus insuring our guests a nice, safe stay in our country. Then, if a visitor decides to move on to another part of the world, our passport mill will give him everything he'll need, including a new identity. For a price, naturally."

Linsey nodded in bored agreement and sipped his beer. He'd heard McCulley's scheme so many times he could have recited it word for word during the rather one-sided conversation. Not that he didn't share his boss's enthusiasm. He was merely sick of hearing about how great everything would be ... *someday*.

Although equally corrupt and almost as ambitious as McCulley, Linsey's background had been entirely different. He'd joined the Navy at the age of seventeen and risen through the ranks to ensign by the time Vietnam got hot. Basically a coward, Linsey managed to avoid any real combat and turned his tour of duty into a profitmaking enterprise by dealing in black market drugs and weapons throughout Southeast Asia, often working with crooked counterparts in the Army and Marine Corps.

After U. S. involvement in 'Nam ended, Linsey nearly got caught in a similar operation in Okinawa and decided to resign from the service. He tried his hand at running a small business in Southern California, but soon encountered trouble from the labor board and the IRS. Thus, he fled to Acapulco and learned to use his nautical

knowledge to become a drug smuggler and gun-
runner in the Gulf of California until McCulley
enlisted him into his scheme. Linsey had the
skills and experience needed for part of the
operation, but he obviously lacked McCulley's
talent as a businessman or financial wizard, thus
he wouldn't turn against his employer—at least
not yet.

"But of course," McCulley began, gazing fondly
at his co-conspirator. "In order to accomplish
our goal we must invade Guadalupe in an incon-
spicuous manner. The idea of forming a fleet of
harmless-looking fishing boats and pleasure craft
was indeed a stroke of genius, if I do say so
myself. However, I could not have accomplished
it without your talents, Joseph." McCulley scooped
some caviar onto a cracker. "Speaking of which,
I believe you have another addition to our
private navy, correct?"

"The thirty-nine foot Newporter," Linsey confirmed. "Got her in dock right now and ready
for a name change and a nice little cruise around
to Honduras."

"Good! Good!" McCulley exclaimed with de-
light.

"Could have been better," Linsey said solemnly.
"There was a real hardass on board the ketch.
Son of a bitch killed three of my men—Woton,
Carter and Josie. Shit! Josie and me go back a
long way. Wouldn't you know it, that little nurd
Jake came out of it without a scratch."

"I'm sorry to hear that," McCulley sighed.
"We can ill afford to lose men at this point. But,
casualties occur in any sort of war. I trust your
men took care of this troublemaker?"

"Caved in his skull and threw him overboard,"

Linsey replied. "What bothers me is we found a briefcase in one of the cuddies on the *Newporter*. It had a .45 automatic—a lightweight Star PD— and three white phosphorous grenades in it."

"Do you think this man may have been some sort of federal agent?" McCulley inquired with a raised eyebrow.

"Could be worse than that," Linsey answered. "A Star PD and 'Willie Peter' grenades sounds like the sort of thing the Penetrator uses and that creep on the boat went through my men like cheap wine through a bum's bladder."

McCulley frowned. He, of course, knew about the Penetrator. He searched his nearly perfect recall for the data. "From what I've heard about the Penetrator," McCulley shrugged, "he appears to act on his own and has no association with any law enforcement organization. In fact, he's wanted in nearly every state in the Union. So what difference does it make? The man is dead and that's the end of it."

"Yeah," Linsey agreed. "I just wish I'd been on board to personally put a bullet in the bastard's head to be sure. The Penetrator is one guy you can't kill *too dead*."

5

Officially Dead

The shark's huge jaws clamped onto the edge of the boat, its long body thrashing in the water as it tried to bite off a chunk of its intended victim. The fish had severely limited intelligence, but an incredible sense of smell that had detected the blood from Clell Brockman's wounded leg. Since it realized the blood was coming from the boat, it attacked the vessel, unable to tell if the target was edible or not until it tried.

Mark Hardin felt the skiff lurch to one side and turned to see the shark holding onto the side, huge triangular teeth lodged in the wooden rim of the dory. The Penetrator tossed another load of water over the side and quickly swung the monkey wrench, striking the shark across the snout. The sensitive nose of a shark is the most vulnerable part of its primitive anatomy. Releasing the skiff, the fish seemed to glare up at Mark with cold, black marble eyes, its evil mouth displaying a vindictive grin.

The Penetrator smashed the wrench over the shark's snout again and the tiger suddenly ducked beneath the waves. Its sleek body shot away from the dory, a long brown-gray blur under the water. Mark glanced at the ocean that surrounded the leaky vessel. More dorsal fins protruded above the surface, cutting great circles as the tiger sharks swam slowly around the disabled skiff, preparing to launch their individual attacks. The promise of food had attracted several other species, the Penetrator noticed with concern. He hoped there were no Great Whites.

Mark and Clell had been fighting off killer fish for almost two hours. The sharks would strike at the boat, hashing into the frame with their great, powerful bodies, gnawing at the wood with enormous jaws that were products of nature's nightmares. Mark and Brockman could only defend themselves by hitting the fish across their noses with the wrench. The finny denizens would then retreat, catch the scent of blood again and swim back for another try.

Mark scooped out more water and threw it out of the dory. The make-do patch job at the bottom of the skiff had begun to leak and the sea fought to win the contest with Mark. He couldn't bail out water and drive off the sharks at the same time. Clell had passed out and lay senseless at the floor of the dory, the tourniquet tied in place and his body partially submerged in seawater.

The Penetrator's arms felt as though they'd been torn from their sockets and painfully stuck back into place with chewing gum. Muscles strained to keep bailing out water, keep fighting off sharks, keep surviving . . .

Suddenly, the sound of wood breaking arrested Mark's attention. Another shark, with a head as big as a boulder, had attacked the boat. Its murderous jaws struck with such force that the fish had literally bitten off a chunk of the skiff. Water poured through the rent and the shark's head pushed its way inside the boat, wicked teeth parted like an entrance to a cave in Hell.

Mark dropped the sea anchor and rose, pulling the wrench from his belt. The shark's head weaved toward Brockman's still form, guided by the smell of the man's blood. Mark swung the wrench with all his dwindling strength, smashing the heavy tool into the fish's nose.

The shark twisted its head toward Mark, moving with uncanny speed for such a large creature. The Penetrator swung again, slamming the implement into one of the dark, bulging fish eyes. The shark's head shifted slightly and Mark hit it a third time on the snout, feeling the vibration of the blow travel up his weary arms.

At last the huge fish retreated back into the ocean, but the ragged tear in the dory had allowed too much water to pour into the boat. Mark waded back to the canvas bailer, splashing through ankle-deep water. He realized it was now hopeless. The sea gushed into the skiff too fast for bailing to do any good. The boat began to sink . . .

The sharp report of a rifle startled the Penetrator.

He turned toward the sound to see a white boat cutting through the sea, a creamy bone in its teeth, with a uniformed figure standing at the bow, working the bolt of a rifle. The Guatamalan Coast Guard patrol boat drew closer and the rifleman fired another shot at the sharks. One of the great fish suddenly twisted in the water, wildly thrashing and struggling amid the waves. Instantly drawn by the scent of fresh blood, the other sharks abandoned the skiff to turn on one of their own.

"Clell!" Mark knelt beside his friend, ignoring the insane splashing of the sharks, caught in a feeding frenzy, and the roar of the rescue boat's engine. "We made it, Clell!" he exclaimed, giddy with relief. "We're gonna be . . ."

The words died in the Penetrator's throat when he saw Clell Brockman's colorless face. Brockman's mouth hung open, the tongue curled back like a shriveled pink tentacle. His eyes stared up at the sun, unblinking, void of life. Mark placed two fingers on the upper lids and forced Clell's eyes to close.

Captain Luis Francisco Sanchez y Ordas sat behind his little metal desk and tried to adjust the long black cheroot in his mouth to avoid having its ash blown all over his clean khaki shirt. It was too hot to do without the large electric fan that circulated an artificial breeze inside the office. Occasionally he became a bit careless and some of the gray powder dusted across his uniform, yet he hardly noticed because the *norteamericano's* story was indeed fascinating and this Mark Hardin spoke excellent Spanish for one born in *los Estados Unidos*.

"I've contacted some friends in my country and they're sending a plane for me," Mark concluded. "I'll also be taking Clell's body back to his family so they can give him a decent funeral."

After a couple of warm meals and six hours

sleep, the Penetrator had fully recovered from his ordeal at sea. Dressed in clean chinos and a borrowed *guayabera*, no one would have guessed he'd recently survived the harrowing experience he'd just reported in detail to Sanchez. In fact, the Guatamalan captain thought the tall, dark American looked like he was ready to take on any tiger shark and tear the creature apart with his bare hands.

"Your tale is quite extraordinary, *Señor* Hardin," Sanchez admitted, blowing a smoke ring at the ceiling. The fan killed it before the thin gray circle could rise past his desk. "I have heard similar stories of pirates from other survivors rescued by our *Guardia Costa*, but we've tended to regard them as amateur boaters who had careless accidents and made up these *piratear cuentos* for insurance purposes."

"*¡Seguro sí!*" Mark responded angrily. "Everybody just happens to come up with the same type of pirate tales and your government doesn't see any connection? *¡Esta desatino!*"

"Señor, Señor," Sanchez appealed, his hands held as though to fend off a physical attack. "I did not mean to suggest that you are being less than truthful. Your friend certainly did not shoot himself and you would not have put yourself in such danger—in a leaky *barca*, surrounded by *los tiburons*—if you had shot him ... not that we suspected you of this, *Señor*."

"*Por supuesto*," the Penetrator allowed. "So what will be done now, *Capitán*?"

Sanchez shrugged. "There is little that can be done. You are a *norteamericano* and so was your friend and the incident occurred more or less in international waters. Officially, it is not a matter for *la Republica de Guatamala*."

"Tell that to my friend," the Penetrator muttered. "But he probably won't hear you. He's officially *dead*."

Dan Griggs met Mark Hardin in the Kaiserhoff, a Bavarian-style restaurant located at the eastern end of Mission Valley in San Diego, off the Waring Road turnoff. Paula, the dirndl-clad co-owner-hostess, escorted them to a table and summoned a waitress to take their order.

Although Mark had conversed with Dan often via telephone, he hadn't actually seen the Justice Department agent in almost two years. He stared at Dan's thinning, iron-gray hair and the wrinkles that had formed at the eyes and mouth. When he'd first met Dan, the man had appeared to be in his late thirties and the gray had barely tinted his temples. Mark suddenly realized Dan must be almost fifty years old.

Dan watched the waitress head for the kitchen before he spoke. "I'm sorry about your friend, Mark."

"Me, too," the Penetrator answered. "Can you help me do something about it?"

The waitress returned with two chilled steins of imported *Ritterbrau Dunkles* beer, the mugs with *Gott mit dir, du Land Bayern* printed on the glass beneath a black German Eagle. An aristocratic looking woman, in traditional Bavarian costume, her white hair asparkle with jeweled combs, began playing an accordian and singing old Bavarian ballads.

"Hell," Dan groaned. "Don't you get into

enough trouble as the Penetrator without starting personal vendettas as well?"

"The pirates started it," Mark insisted. "I intend to finish it."

"Okay," the Justice man sighed. He took a long sip of *Dunkles* before he spoke. "I checked into that business about hijacking boats. It's been happening in the Gulf of Mexico even more often than on the West Coast. The whole scam has been going on for a long time now, you know."

"Yeah," Mark agreed. "Professor Haskins ran the data through his computers at the Stronghold. There's been a big increase in such hijackings in recent months."

"I know. Some of the boats are winding up in the hands of drug smugglers. Since the Mexican *peso* took a nose dive the border patrol and the narcotics boys have had their hands full. A lot of *coyotes* are getting bolder and trying extra hard to run wetbacks and dope into the U. S. and guns back to Mexico for big *gringo* bucks."

"The Professor's sources covered that, too," Mark stated. "But the drug traffic doesn't explain the increase in blue water pleasure boats being grabbed by pirates. A big white yacht is too conspicuous for smugglers to use. It has to be something else."

"Any idea what that something might be?" Dan inquired.

"Not yet," the Penetrator admitted. "But I'm going to find out."

"Don't you always?" Dan sighed.

The waitress returned with their meals—two *Wurstplatte* of *Weisswurst*, *Brattwurst* and *Le-*

berkase liver sausage, hard black bread and boiled vegetables. Dan waited for the girl to leave before he reached inside his conservative gray suit jacket and extracted a leather ID case.

"This might help," he said, handing it to Mark. "It'll identify you as James Banner of the Organized Crime Network of the Justice Department."

"Thanks, Dan," the Penetrator nodded, taking the ID.

"You'll also find something new and different in there," the Justice man remarked. "A federal gun permit. Cuts the red tape of taking a firearm on board an airliner. Might save you some hassle if you'd get used to carrying one, you know."

Mark grinned. "Still trying to recruit me?"

"Might not be a bad idea," Dan returned solemnly. "How long do you think you can keep doing this 'lone crusader' stuff, Mark? Hell, I'm going to retire in a few more years and Willard Haskins isn't getting any younger either."

The Penetrator mentally winced. Professor Haskins was approaching his eightieth birthday. And, what about David Red Eagle? The medicine chief had been an incredibly old man when Mark had first met him. How old, even David didn't know for sure, though he maintained he had been a young boy at the time of the massacre of the Cheyenne at the Washita. No one lives forever and all of his colleagues, even Dan, would soon be out of the "Penetrating" picture. What would he do then? How would he cope with the loss of his closest friends, people who had virtually become his family over the years?

"Didn't mean to upset you, Mark," Dan assured him, startled by the expression of total bewilderment that had fleetingly appeared on his friend's face. "Just something to think about, that's all."

"I have been," the Penetrator replied quietly, pocketing the ID folder.

6

Pirates of Fortune

Deep in the Honduran jungle, near the east coast of the country, men screamed war whoops and curses in half a dozen languages. Green uniformed figures dashed toward a number of crudely made structures, consisting of poles driven into the ground with "walls" made of fishnetting. The soldiers fired their weapons—mostly AKM and M-16 assault rifles, although a few had Uzis and two men carried old MP-40 "Schmeisser" submachine guns—while they approached.

The soldiers moved in a swift, well-coordinated manner. They worked in teams and supplied cover fire for each other when attacking. No one bunched up or drifted too far from the others. An M-80 simulator exploded in front of the assault force. A few curses were the only response. None of the men panicked or hesitated. Another M-80 went off. One of the soldiers lobbed a cannister at a "building." It bounced off the netting and a cloud of dense green smoke soon hissed from the grenade.

Everyone continued forward. Something sizzled over their heads, but no one paid much attention. The mortar round crashed into an isolated stick-net structure and exploded, tearing the flimsy "building" to pieces. The soldiers kept moving until each team had claimed its goal, eliminating the remaining huts.

Contrary to its appearance, this was not a training camp for a contingent of the leftist terrorists who had plagued Central America over the past few years. These men were pros.

Colonel Treaver Jacoby raised a bullhorn and spoke through it. "That's fine men," his amplified, tinny voice announced. "Take ten."

The soldiers gratefully obeyed and shuffled from the clearing in the rain forest that contained the mock town. Jacoby, a tall, broad-shouldered man with a great handlebar mustache and dark blue eyes, turned to offer a wry smile to his visitors.

"Went quite nicely," he stated, his British accent giving the "c" in "nicely" a long "s" sound. "Don't you agree, Mr. McCulley?"

The fat man mopped his forehead with a sweat-stained handkerchief. "Do they have to use so much blank ammunition?" Kimberly McCulley complained. "My computers didn't calculate this as a necessary expense in the training operations."

"Computers are machines," Jacoby replied flatly. "They can only handle what's been programed into them. Unless you had a military man feed data into them, you can't expect the information to be complete."

"I helped to program the computers," Joe Linsey stated, scraping a thumbnail inside a nostril.

Jacoby watched with distaste while Linsey wiped the snot on his trousers. "That rather confirms what I said, doesn't it?" the colonel remarked dryly.

"I spent almost twenty years in the Navy," Linsey declared, stung by Jacoby's insult. "I was in Vietnam, damn it."

"But you were never much of a military man, were you?" Jacoby looked at Linsey with utter disdain.

"Fuck you," Linsey replied for lack of any comeback.

"No need to get offensive, Joseph," McCulley sad.

"He started it, Kim," Linsey pouted as he fished a pack of cigarettes out of his pocket.

"Must you smoke?" McCulley grimaced.

"Yeah, I must," Linsey responded, flicking his butane Cricket.

"Firing blank ammunition, the simulators and the live mortar rounds are all part of realistic combat training," Jacoby explained to McCulley, choosing to ignore Linsey whom he regarded as a contemptible renegade.

Jacoby had served in the British Army for thirty-five years. He'd seen action in the Suez and Cyprus and had been awarded the Military Cross, the United Nations Service Medal and the Medal of Valor. He'd retired from the service, not because he had to avoid the discovery of illegal activities like Linsey, but because he'd been put behind a desk and ordered to command paperwork. Jacoby had still craved action, but the high mucky-mucks, who couldn't even handle riff-raff from the IRA, thought he was too old for combat commands.

Thus, Col. Treavor Jacoby became a mercenary. To be more precise, he became a mercenary commander. Jacoby had acquired numerous connections during his military career and he used them to recruit almost 150 European soldiers for hire. These same connections helped him find clients in Africa and the Middle East. One quality Jacoby shared with his current partners was a lack of principles. He had been willing to fight for whoever paid the bills—Saudi Arabia or Libya, Rhodesia or Angola. McCulley had money and, if his scheme succeeded, he'd have considerably more in the future. To Jacoby, this made him an ideal client.

"Where'd you hide the yachts, *Colonel*?" Linsey inquired, using Jacoby's title as though it were an insult. "Didn't blow 'em up by accident, did you?"

Jacoby glared at him. "The boats are in a yacht basin—which is a perfectly logical place for them and won't attract any undue attention—on Laguna de Credasco. That connects with the Caribbean, in case you've never smuggled any narcotics around this area during your checkered career, *Mister* Linsey."

"We're using a tourist promotional deal for a cover, Joseph," McCulley explained, trying to prevent an argument between the two men. "It was my idea. The slogan is 'Rent a beach house and a yacht in Paradise.' The Honduran government loves it and no one suspects a thing."

"That's right, Linsey," Jacoby smiled. "I'll take care of the boats after you get them to us and see that they're used for what I know best ... fighting other men in combat. You just do what *you* do best and keep stealing them for us."

Linsey's eyes narrowed. "I hope you know what you're doing, Kim. This Limey windbag and his toy soldiers are supposed to take an entire country. Sure, it isn't much of a country, but they're not going to find it as easy as blowing away a bunch of niggers in the Congo or whatever this guy is used to doing."

"The island of Guadalupe is *not* a country," Jacoby stated firmly. "It is a French protectorate and thereby, it will present relatively little challenge for my personal army of professional soldiers."

"Yeah," Linsey snickered. "I bet Argentina figured the British would just sit back and let the spics have the Falkland Islands, too."

"The French are not the British," Jacoby retorted. "I ought to know. Besides, France has enough problems at home these days. Thanks to their current Socialist government, domestic unrest and the economy are a national headache, not to mention the increase of terrorist activity and trouble from various radical political outfits. No, Linsey, the French will keep out of the Caribbean."

"The colonel's right, Joseph," McCulley declared. "My computers back him up. But, you're both wrong to quarrel so. We're all about to reap the rewards of the most ambitious privately organized invasion of the twentieth century." Beaming, he glanced around the mercenary training camp.

It had cost a small fortune to establish it here in the jungles of Honduras, but it had been worth the expense and bribes. His dream of conquest and power would soon become a reality.

"Nothing can stop us," McCulley whispered. "Absolutely nothing."

*   *   *

Mark Hardin sat under the canopy of the Atlantis Cafe, located on a harbor in Galveston. People who think of Texas as consisting entirely of cowboys, cattle, oil wells and J. R. Ewing, have never been to Galveston. Situated on the Intercoastal Waterway along the Gulf of Mexico, Galveston is the main seaport of the Lone Star State. The Penetrator had selected it as the starting point for his search for the yacht pirates.

Both Professor Haskins' sources and the Justice Department's information indicated that most of the hijackings had been boats that set out from the Galveston-to-New Orleans area. While he consumed an excellent lunch of steak and shrimp, Mark reflected on his uneventful visit to the Galveston Coast Guard office. The local authorities had been eager to assist "James Banner" of the OCN, but they had nothing to add to what he'd already discovered about the hijackings.

The Penetrator could apparently scratch Galveston as a possible lead. Next he'd check the Bolivar Penninsula and then the Sabine Pass that separates Texas and Louisiana. He mentally groaned when he thought of the coastal area that would still remain to be investigated. The Chandeler and Breton Sound and Lake Pontchartrain, the Mississippi delta, not to mention numerous passes and riverways in between. If none of those turned up any clues, then Mark would have to try Mississippi, moving eastward through Georgia to Florida. Or the Gulf of California . . . or buy a Ouija board.

Mark sipped his iced tea and watched the seagulls circle above the waves, occasionally diving low to pluck some bread from the water. A

couple of young kids standing on the pier tossed
food to the birds. Two somewhat older boys
were fishing with cheap rods and reels, their
lines dangling over the rail of a small foot bridge.
A large commercial shrimp boat slowly trudged
out to sea and two blue water boats sailed grace-
fully along the sun-laced water.

The Penetrator would have enjoyed the scene
under different circumstances, but everything
reminded him of his self-appointed mission and
the murder of Clell Brockman. Yet, what proof
did he have of a conspiracy? *Neptune's Dream*,
the real name of the trawler that had attacked
them, had been missing for almost a week before the incident and could easily have fallen
into the hands of smugglers who wanted the *All
American* for reasons of their own.

Perhaps Clell's rich, ex-football player client
had a stash of coke hidden on the yacht. Hell,
Mark didn't really know Clell Brockman well
enough to be certain his old college chum wasn't
transporting dope himself. Maybe he was bark-
ing up the wrong proverbial tree. Perhaps, this
time, he should let the authorities handle the
matter.

The wail of a siren drew Mark's attention to
the center of the pier where a white and red
ambulance had suddenly screeched to a halt.
Two paramedics hopped out and scrambled to
the back of the vehicle to unload two gurneys.
The children and a couple of adults abandoned
their individual activities and approached the
paramedics. The youngsters asked what had
happened. More than one voice seemed eager to
hear about a disaster, the bloodier the better.

"Coast Guard's bringing in a couple of people

who had a boating accident," one of the paramedics explained. "Please stand back and give
us enough room to do our job, okay?"

Mark's pulse quickened when he heard the
reply. He paid for his meal and strolled over to
the pier, warning himself not to jump to conclusions. The whirling sound of huge blades chopping air drew everyone's attention to the big
white Bell HH-1K helicoptor that appeared over
the ocean. Designed for sea rescue and equipped
with a powerful Lycoming T53-L13 engine, the
Coast Guard chopper quickly flew over the harbor and hovered above the pier.

The paramedics and their gurneys moved in
when the Bell's amphibious landing gear began
to touch down. A pair of Coast Guard officers
escorted two haggard figures, a man and a
woman, from the helicopter. The couple wore
shrouds made of thick blue blankets. They shook
their heads when they saw the stretchers. Mark
recognized one of the officers, a rugged, sun-
tanned lieutenant named Buchner, whom he'd
spoken to earlier about the hijackings. Buchner
said something to the paramedics and they
agreed to allow the couple to walk to the ambulance.

While the medical attendants and the rescued
couple climbed into the vehicle, Mark approached
the chopper. The pilot had killed the engine
and the great blades were slowly revolving, the
noise reduced considerably. Mark called out to
Buchner.

"Hullo. Mr. Banner, isn't it?" the lieutenant
greeted. "Glad to see you again. Might save us
both some time."

"Another boat-napping?" Mark inquired.

Buchner nodded. "Mr. and Mrs. Zanther rented a yacht, a thirty-nine footer, and set out for a little pleasure cruise yesterday. Signed on a kid to crew for them. They're sailing around, exactly where they were they can only guess, when another yacht shows up. Same MO as before. The pirates on board the other vessel claimed they needed help, the Zanthers agreed to let a couple of the guys on their boat and the bastards pulled guns on them."

"They were lucky," the Penetrator declared. "Sometimes the pirates appear to kill first and steal later."

"The Zanthers weren't injured," Buchner said. "Oh, they were pretty worn out and hungry and they might have a touch of pneumonia after spending the night drifting around in a lifeboat. They were afraid it'd be worse. According to them, the hijackers were a mean-looking bunch commanded by a bearded guy with a German pistol. Zanther thinks it was a Luger or something like one. They said one of the pirates wasn't much smaller than a California Redwood and had crazy eyes like some sort of drug freak. Oh, the kid they signed on wasn't so lucky."

"Did the pirates kill him?" Mark asked grimly.

"Took him captive for some reason," Buchner replied, leafing through a note pad. "We'll have to check the kid out. He told the Zanthers his name was Richard Dennis, but so many of these beach bum types are runaways that it could be a phony."

Mark managed to conceal the sudden enlightenment that hit him in the brain like a mental hammer. Brockman had hired a kid—Dennis Richards—and the Zanthers had signed on *Rich-*

ard Dennis. Of course, he thought. He promised to kick himself later, when no one would see him do it, for not realizing what had happened aboard the *All American* until now.

The punk had been an accomplice. That explained why Dennis hadn't been thrown overboard with Mark and Clell and why the pirates had "captured" the little fraud after seizing the Zanther boat. It also told Mark who had hit him over the head during the gun battle with the hijackers on board the *All American.* He'd wondered how the lone survivor of the pirate crew had managed to sneak up behind him. Dennis or Richard or whoever the junior louse really was had done it.

"I've got to fill out some paperwork, Mr. Banner," Buchner said. "You want to come along and get the rest of the details?"

"Not right now," the Penetrator replied. "I've got to check out a couple of other things first. Thanks for all your help."

He walked away from the helicopter and wondered what sort of wardrobe beach bums favored these days. If he was going to comb the Galveston-to-New Orleans area looking for Dennis-the-Punk, he'd better try a new role and look and act accordingly. What the hell do beach bums do, anyway?

"Panhandle for sea shells," Mark muttered under his breath, answering his own question as he strolled from the pier.

7

After Dinner Death

Joe Linsey lit a marijuana cigarette and took a long toke, drawing the smoke deep into his lungs. Lousy shit, he thought. He'd had better stuff back in 'Nam. They'd had such a beautiful black market ring going in those days, until some of the Army guys screwed up. A fucking boy scout sergeant named Mark Hardin got wind of their operation and blew the whistle on them. God-damned snoop got his brains kicked out for it later on, but the ring was still ruined.

Knuckles rapped harshly on the door of his hotel room. Christ, he thought. Couldn't be the cops. No way they'd be wise to him in New Orleans. Not the feds either. They don't move that fast. Hilton is a respectable hotel chain and that meant they might have a sharp house detective in the place. Great. There he was in the front room with a dube in one hand, a *Hustler* magazine in the other and his pants pulled down to his ankles. Not to mention a throbbing hard-on.

Dropping the magazine, Linsey almost tripped over his trousers before he remembered to yank them up. He awkwardly dashed to the bathroom, tossed the joint into the toilet and flushed it away. Burial at sea. He'd whistle "Taps" for it later. The knocking at the door turned into fist-pounding. Crap. Whoever it was, he meant business. Linsey jogged back to the front room and spotted his Walther P-38 on the coffee table beside a can of beer.

"Just a minute," he yelled at the door.

Quickly he stuffed the pistol under the seat cushion of his chair and headed for the door. Slipping the chain latch, he turned the knob. The panel popped open before he could pull it and the rat-like face of Jake Lieter suddenly appeared.

"Aw, fuck," Linsey moaned, thinking of the Mexican grass he'd flushed down the john. "What'a you want?"

"We got problems, Joe," Jake declared, hurrying into the room and shutting the door.

"Yeah. I'm looking at one of mine," Linsey snorted. "What is it?"

"A guy's been snoopin' around, Joe," Jake explained. "He's been hangin' around the boat-yards in Galveston, Rene Pointe, Breton Sound and now he's here in New Orleans. He's been askin' questions. Tryin' to find a kid named Dennis or Richard . . ."

Linsey's jaw tightened. "Are you sure it's the same guy every time?"

"The description I've gotten from our men is always the same," Jake answered. "Tall, dark guy with black hair and lots of muscles. A couple of the boys say he looks like he's part greaser or maybe Indian or somethin'."

"Have you seen him yet?"

"Well, no . . ."

"I want you to get a good look at this son of a bitch, Jake," Linsey thrust a finger at his flunky. "I want to know if he's the same character you and Dennis tossed in the drink a while back."

"You mean the one who killed Josie, Carter and Woton?" Jake shivered, recalling the incident on the *All American*.

"That's right," Linsey returned sternly.

"But we killed him, Joe!"

"Oh, yeah?" Linsey answered with a sneer. "Then who the fuck do you think it was who reported the hijacking of that boat and the killing of that yacht broker? That's the reason McCulley wants us to handle all our boat grabbing with kid gloves. 'Can't have any more reports of murder on the high seas,' the fat fart says. 'Don't want the authorities on us now that we're so close to completion of our plans.' Shit. That new rule has made it a bitch and a half to get new boats."

"So you want me to get a good look at this guy, Joe?" inquired the slow-witted henchman.

"I don't want you to *look* at him, asshole," Linsey snapped. "I want you to kill him! This ain't the high seas so McCulley can go fuck himself. I'm gonna contact Redfield and put him in charge of the hit. He's done this sort of thing before. I want three, maybe four more guys in on this too. I want it done *right* this time."

"Six of us to take care of one man?" Jake's eyes bulged from his dull face.

"You heard right, numb-nuts!" Linsey growled. He didn't dare tell Jake the truth. Sending half a dozen assassins isn't at all unreasonable . . . when their target may well be the Penetrator.

*   *   *

Dressed in a single-breasted dark blue suit and carrying an attaché case, Mark Hardin appeared to be a busy young executive who'd just had dinner with a client at *Le Bon Creole*, one of the finest restaurants in the French Quarter of New Orleans.

The Penetrator glanced at his wristwatch. Nine thirty-five. A rather late dinner, but he'd been running a somewhat unorthodox schedule. Beach bums don't keep regular hours and his disguise had required him to mingle with various types of fishermen, wharf rats and left-over hippies who hadn't heard that the anarchy of the sixties was no longer in fashion.

After five days of wandering around harbors and beaches, dressed in cut-offs, sandals and a fishnet T-shirt, Mark learned fishermen were generous with beer and usually friendly enough, but they generally kept out of other people's business and noticed little that didn't seem to concern them. The over aged rebels without a cause were still as worthless as ever, unless one wanted information about where to buy drugs or cared to listen to simplistic anti-establishment hogwash.

However, the harbor hoboes proved to be of some value. Like the winos of the cities, many of the pier-bound tramps had discovered that by keeping their eyes and ears open, they could learn bits of information that would be worth the price of a cheap bottle of Sweet Lucy. Stevedores looking for work, street whores in search of johns, smugglers seeking a quiet place to make a trade and feds hunting for the smugglers had all made such business deals for Tokay wine with the wharf rats.

A kid named Richard or Dennis? Slender? Long hair? Sort of an Arkansas accent? Some of the hoboes had seen him around, looking for scut work on those fancy white yachts, the type good-for-nothin' rich folks play around in, one put it. Another tramp recalled that the kid had been hired and left in a boat out of Breton Sound, but he hadn't seen the youth since and wasn't certain if the yacht had returned or not. After all, they all looked alike. Others only remembered seeing Dennis Richard around various piers and weren't sure if he'd left as the crew of any boats.

By the third day, Mark began to notice men standing at a distance with open newspapers and fishermen who neglected to bring a bucket for their catch or even to bait their hooks. Someone had taken an interest in the Penetrator's activities. This neither surprised nor alarmed him. Mark realized he was a conspicuous individual and the fact that he was being tailed meant his quarry might decide to come to him, which would save a lot of time and effort. So he allowed the shadows to tag along and believe he remained ignorant of their intentions. Sooner or later, the opposition would make its move.

Yet hanging around the docks had become tiresome and unproductive. Confident the tails would follow, he decided to abandon the beach bum routine and enjoy some of New Orleans' famous cuisine.

Mark walked from *Le Bon Creole*, cautiously glancing at passersby. None of them appeared to offer any threat or suggested any undue interest in him. Paranoia is an extremely real risk for anyone involved in clandestine-style operations and this especially applied to the Penetrator,

who handled missions no undercover cop or co-
vert government agent would ever dream of. He
realized that while he could never afford to be
unalert, he couldn't allow himself to start jumping at shadows either.

The Penetrator strolled to an indoor parking lot three blocks from the restaurant, at the
corner of Toulouse and Rampart. He remained
keenly alert when he entered. The files of cars,
lined up in neat rows, might easily conceal an
ambush. His footsteps echoed inside the concrete cavern, developing a sinister quality to his
suspicious ear.

A young black couple walked hand-in-hand
from a yellow Datsun while a somewhat older
man and wife escorted three tow-headed young
children from a white Cadillac. Wearily consult-
ing a clipboard, a gray-haired lot attendant
checked the tickets jammed under windshield
wipers to be certain no one had somehow smuggled a car inside without paying first.

"Good evenin', suh," the old man greeted, his
wrinkled ebony face managing a weak, toothless
smile.

Mark returned the hello and continued into
the lot. The place was filthy. Bags of garbage
and unsheathed piles of trash lined the walls
and filled the corners of the building. Graffiti,
containing obscenities in English, French and
Spanish, decorated the walls and pillars. The
stench of rotten food, stale beer and human ex-
crement assaulted Mark's nostrils—and for the
Quarter, this parking lot was cleaner than most.

At last he located his rented dark blue Mazda.
Could someone have planted a bomb in the car?
Possible, but not likely. The lot attendant would

be apt to notice anyone monkeying around with an automobile and if the would-be assassin didn't have a ticket that matched the number on the clipboard, he'd have a hard time explaining his actions. Since the attendant appeared to be alive and well—and genuine—Mark fished his keys out of a pocket and approached the car.

Two shadows suddenly rose up from the nose of the Mazda and rushed toward the Penetrator. Steel flashed in the assailants' fists as they attacked. Mark heard a third opponent running toward him from the rear, but he concentrated his attention on the two closer adversaries—and hoped number three wasn't about to put a bullet in his back.

The Penetrator swiftly raised his attaché case to meet the knife thrust of the first man. Steel connected with the tough Samsonite luggage, deflecting the blade. Mark saw the startled face of his wide-eyed, flat-nosed opponent an instant before he struck out with his other hand, holding the car keys firmly between thumb and bent forefinger.

Hard metal stabbed into the thug's throat, crushing his thyroid cartilage and shutting off his windpipe. The knife artist dropped his weapon and staggered backward into his partner, clutching his ruined throat with both hands while blood vomited from his open mouth.

Mark half-saw, half-sensed the lashing arm of the hood closing in from behind. He weaved out of the path of a knife slash, feeling the blade tug the sleeve of his suit jacket. The Penetrator's foot shot out in a low side kick, the edge of his shoe striking the would-be assassin's shin. The man stumbled slightly and Mark whirled to swing the attaché case upward, driving a hard corner into his opponent's solar plexus.

While the hood gasped breathlessly and began to double up from the blow, Mark dropped his car keys and plucked a Guardfather from the lapel pocket of his suit. The manufacturers at Brygs, Incorporated in Georgia must have wondered why he'd ordered two dozen of their "push-button ice-picks." The Penetrator then lived up to his name. When the thick steel spike shot out and locked in place, he promptly stabbed the point through the killer's left eyesocket to *penetrate* his brain.

Hal Brandon, the third ambusher, shoved his dead partner aside and rushed in, trying to jab the point of his switchblade under Mark's ribcage. The Penetrator blocked the thrust with his briefcase and quickly swung it in a vicious backhand sweep. The sturdy valise slammed across Brandon's pockmarked, bearded face and sent him sprawling along the side of a Dodge Dart parked next to Mark's car.

Mark could have plunged the Guardfather into Brandon's exposed kidneys, but he wanted the man alive for interrogation. The Penetrator swung his attaché case again, chopping the edge into Brandon's wrist above the switchblade. The knife clattered on the paved floor and the thug stared up at Mark, his face a pale mask of terror.

Shoe leather slapping concrete alerted the Penetrator in time to see three more figures rapidly advancing—all of them carrying guns! He immediately threw himself onto the hood of the Mazda, kicking hard to execute a fast backward roll to the other side of the car. A shot bellowed and echoed within the enclosed lot.

Glass shattered in the rear window of the Mazda, but the bullet failed to find its swift human target.

Crouched behind the car, the Penetrator drew a Safari Arms .45 caliber MatchMaster from a shoulder holster. Like the Guardfather, the pistol was a relatively new addition to his "Penetrating" arsenal, yet he'd been very pleased with its accuracy on the firing range and it had served him well on a recent mission to Nicaragua. The trio of gunmen began to fan out to surround the Mazda. Almost casually, Mark flicked off the pistol's ambidexterous safety catch, aimed the MatchMaster and fired.

A big 185 grain JHP bullet plowed into the chest of the closest gunman. The heavy slug kicked the man's body backward to crash unceremoniously to the concrete. The other hoods scrambled for cover. Amid the echo of the .45's boom, a woman screamed and one of the hired killers growled, "Christ, he's got heat!"

The oracle of this rather obvious truth was Carson Redfield. A blocky, square-faced thug who'd lived twenty-seven years too long, Redfield had graduated from street gangs and petty larceny to freelance hitman until he'd been hired by Joe Linsey six months before. Redfield, who regarded himself a fearless professional, now found himself cowering behind a Ford Pinto with a skinned knee and a frost-covered backbone.

Jake Leiter knelt beside him, violently trembling, hardly able to hold his .38 snubnosed revolver in his shaky hands. Wondering if he looked as bad, Redfield was shamed into regaining his self-control. He tightened his grip on his own

.380 Beretta automatic and waited until he could trust his teeth not to chatter before he spoke.

"Get a hold of yourself, Jake!" he snapped. "So the first team failed to take this guy quietly. Now we gotta do it. We've still got the bastard out-numbered."

"He moves like fuckin' lightning," Jake rasped. "It *is* the same guy!"

"Whadda ya mean? Who is this guy?"

"Sudden death on two feet."

"Shit," Redfield spat through a sneer. "To listen to you, a guy'd think we was after the Penetrator or somethin' . . ."

Both men turned sharply when they heard someone scramble to their position. They almost opened fire before they recognized the ugly face of Hal Brandon. Getting swatted in the mouth with a Samsonite attaché case hadn't improved his appearance. Blood trickled from a split lip to form a crimson line to his mangey beard.

"Hal!" Jake exclaimed. "We were afraid he got all three of you."

Redfield wasn't nearly so pleased to discover Brandon still alive. "Goddamn fuck ups! Couldn't manage to take one guy!"

"Son of a bitch is a regular tiger, Red," Brandon said thickly. "Let's get outta here. The cops are gonna show up soon . . . if that hardass don't waste us first."

"You're already a waste," Redfield muttered. He pulled up a pantleg and drew a .22 caliber High Standard Double Nine revolver from an ankle holster. "Try not to shoot yourself, dipshit."

Reluctantly, Hal took the gun.

"Okay," Redfield continued. "Don't bunch up.

It'll be tougher for him if he's got three targets to deal with. Don't spread out too far either. We got plenty of cover with all these cars. Once we pin the sucker down, we'll have no sweat blastin' his ass and gettin' out of here before the oinkers can get their fuzzmobiles in gear."

The Penetrator had changed position, surreptitiously creeping to the cover of a Buick stationwagon parked in a row twenty yards from his Mazda. He watched the trio scurry forward, but held his fire because no clear target had been offered. Hide and seek with guns, he thought grimly.

Soon, Brandon oozed into an aisle and moved between a pickup truck and a Ford Galaxy 500 parked next to the Buick. Mark purposely rose up and ducked down to get the man's attention. Brandon whirled and fired two rapid shots at the fleeting movement. The .22 rounds pinged off concrete somewhere beyond the cars.

"You almost shot me, you idiot!" Mark shouted angrily.

Hal Brandon blinked with surprise, wondering how one of his partners had managed to get to a position so far from where he'd left them. He lowered the Double Nine peashooter and raised his head.

"Red?" he called out softly.

The Penetrator appeared at the hood of the Buick, the MatchMaster held in a two-handed Weaver's grip and aimed at Brandon's voice. The dull-witted thug's mouth sagged open as he realized he'd been tricked. Then Mark shot him in the face.

Brandon's nose transformed into a scarlet

smear and the back of his head burst apart like a rotten cabbage smacked by a sledge hammer.

Redfield and Jake dashed from their cover, both firing at the Penetrator's position. A .380 round whined when it richocheted off the steel frame of the Buick and one of Jake's .38 slugs shattered the window by the wagon's driver's seat. They scrambled forward from opposite sides and approached the Buick carefully, one man at each end of the car. Their quarry had disappeared.

"The guy's a goddamned ghost," Jake whispered with awe.

"Put a couple of bullets in him and he'll die like anybody else," Redfield growled, trying to sound more confident than he felt.

"If he doesn't get us first," Jake whined.

"Shut up!" Redfield snapped. "Come on. Let's get the fucker."

Once again the gunmen split up and slinked between parked vehicles, moving from row to row. Jake Lieter slipped into a space with a Chevy sedan on one side and a Ford camper on the other. He licked his lips with a sandpaper-dry tongue and clenched the .38 tightly in his sweat-soaked fist. Goddamn Linsey! He'd said this business would be a cakewalk from start to finish. Hijacking yachts from stuck-up rich bastards was one thing, but shoot-outs with a professional badass wasn't ...

Suddenly something skidded from under the camper and slid in front of Jake's feet. He jerked back with a start and then stared down at the attaché case, totally confused. Then he remembered that the hardcase had such a valise and turned his attention to the front of the camper, pointing his revolver in the same direction.

When he failed to spot his adversary he began to turn. The Penetrator, crouched by the rear of the camper, shot him in the chest.

Jake saw the flash of Mark's MatchMaster, heard it roar and felt the heavy .45 caliber slug tear into his body. His back slammed into the Chevy and he fired his revolver into the side of the camper. Mark drilled another round through the hood's scrawny chest and Jake Leiter slid to the pavement and died.

"Jake?" Redfield called.

The silence that followed served as an answer.

When the wail of sirens followed, Carson Redfield decided it was time to get out of there. Whoever the triggerman might be—Jesus! It could even be the Penetrator! He was too much to deal with all by himself without having the cops around as well. Redfield slithered through the columns of vehicles and worked his way to the entrance of the lot.

Mark Hardin watched the thug emerge from the rows of cars and followed his progress, keeping Redfield over the sights of his MatchMaster pistol. The howling siren grew louder and the hood suddenly bolted into the open.

Mark aimed carefully and squeezed the trigger.

The Safari Arms blaster boomed and the .45 caliber projectile sliced through the air and found exactly the target the Penetrator wanted. The bullet hit Redfield in the left thigh, pierced flesh and muscle and snapped the bone beneath like a dry tree branch struck by lightning.

The hitman cried out in surprise and pain. Redfield fell to the pavement as though slapped down by an invisible giant's hand. He sprawled on his belly and the Beretta flew from his grasp to skid ten feet beyond the killer's reach.

"Tag," Mark said, pleased that he'd been able to take one of the hoods alive. "You're it."

Then twin headlights knifed into the parking lot, followed by a big blue and white vehicle with flashing lights mounted on its roof. The insane wail of the siren filled the enclosed area like a banshee in a nightmare. The New Orleans police officer behind the wheel failed to notice Carson Redfield's prone figure in time.

He hit the brake a split second too late and felt the car rise up and come down when the tires rolled over the man's body.

"Awh, shit!" The Penetrator groaned as he shoved his MatchMaster back into its shoulder holster.

8

All Grown Up

Lt. Frank Hayward looked at Carson Redfield's blood-splattered, hideously crushed body and shook his head with dismay. Hayward was with the Public Information Office of the New Orleans Department of Police. He had been in the Quarter in regard to arrangements for a motion picture company and had answered the call as the most senior officer near the scene. A competent investigator, he also had more than one interest in the case. And this one was going to be a real pain in the ass. Nuts!

A multiple slaying by a single person would be hard enough to handle from the standpoint of the press. But he had arrived at the parking garage to discover that one of the Department's own vehicles was about to become as infamous as Ted Kennedy's green sedan.

Hayward knew about Redfield, Brandon and a couple of the other low-lifes who'd caught bullets in the lot and the others were probably out-of-town scum—as if the city needed to import any. The guy who'd helped rid New Orleans of some two-bit vermin appeared to be a hotshot fed from the Justice Department. Although his credentials seemed in order, there was something funny about this James Banner.

The Penetrator watched Hayward approach. The cop looked like a linebacker for the Rams, almost as tall as Mark, powerfully built, with broad shoulders and a barrel chest that seemed to start just below the chin and end a bit above the crotch. Hayward's upper torso seemed to roll when he walked across the parking lot, which now contained more police than a Dunkin' Donuts on a Monday night.

"They must train you guys mighty well at the Justice Department," the cop commented in a tenor voice that revealed only a trace of the faintly Brooklyn-like accent of a native of New Orleans. "Took out six armed men. Impressive."

"Five," Mark corrected. "Your man in the car . . ."

"Don't remind me," Hayward muttered. A frown appeared on his round face and some of the twinkle left his blue eyes for a moment. "That's a lot of guys involved in a mugging. Are you sure that's all they were—muggers?"

"Lieutenant," the Penetrator sighed. "I've already explained that I'm here to investigate alleged drug traffic involving Carlo Santucci's Mafia family. I've only scratched the surface so far and, sorry to say, I haven't gotten deep enough into the investigation to merit anyone sending half a dozen gunmen to waste me. I also haven't accomplished enough to have my presence here made public."

"Uh-huh." Hayward nodded. "Did you know Carson Redfield, the human pancake over there, worked as a gun for hire?"

"Like Paladin, huh?" Mark grinned. "No, I

didn't know about the guy. We never got around to exchanging introductions."

"Why do you suppose a hitman would be operating with a bunch of muggers?"

"A lot of people have to work two jobs these days with the economy in the shape it is," the Penetrator remarked. "Come on, Lieutenant. How would you expect a two-bit buttonman to make money between hits? Selling Christmas cards? Going door to door for Avon?"

"Got a point," Hayward allowed. "We'll have to take you to the center. Ask for a written statement. Maybe check your ID with Washington and the serial numbers on your gun and your fingerprints."

"That's fine with me, Lieutenant, check away," the Penetrator replied. Dan Griggs had already filed all that information into the Justice Department computers. On every mission Mark wore specially made ultra-thin rubber gloves that could not be detected by looking at his hands or touching them. The fingerprints engraved on this set would match the DOJ file on "James Banner."

"Okay." Hayward smiled thinly. "Say, you pack a .45 MatchMaster, right? I hear it's a good piece. Read about it in a gun magazine a while back. You ever handle a Colt Commander? How about a Star PD?" A bushy eyebrow rose to emphasize the questions.

"Hell," Mark returned with a shrug. "I've gotten to use a lot of different types of firearms on the range."

"Uh-huh," the cop sighed. "On the firing range. Sure."

The Penetrator went with Hayward to the De-

partment of Police Headquarters where he spent
the rest of the night and part of the morning
answering questions and signing statements.
Fortunately, Mark's OCN ID and the fact a
patrolcar, driven by one of New Orleans' finest,
had run over one of the "muggers" encouraged
the cops to favor his story and agree to put a lid
on some of the details for a while.

Naturally, everyone—especially Mark and
Frank Hayward—realized the incident had been
more than a simple attempted mugging with a
happy ending for the intended "muggee," but
nobody could get too upset about a clutch of
hoods killed in self-defense. Hayward obviously
suspected Mark's true identity. However, the
cop— like many other law enforcement personnel—didn't really disapprove of the Penetrator,
and Hayward probably wouldn't lean on "James
Banner" unless the Department forced his hand.
This meant Mark had to wrap up business in
New Orleans and move on as quickly as possible.

"Welcome to Fan-tasy Island," Mark Hardin
remarked under his breath when he caught a
glimpse of his reflection in the window of *Le
Bibelots*, a novelty shop located along the east
side of Jackson Square.

Dressed in a light-weight, white suit with a
black tie, the Penetrator hadn't decided to im-
personate Ricardo Montalban, it only looked that
way. Because his role as a beach bum had gained
little and his cover as "James Banner" was now
in jeopardy, it became time to change tactics. So,
Mark had adopted a new disguise as a prospec-
tive yacht buyer.

He strolled past the French Market to a small

marina, going from slip to slip, asking questions about the price of yachts and where to lease or buy them. He wanted to know their handling characteristics and where to hire a crew if needed. He specified any kid fresh out of high school who'd be interested in a little extra cash. The entire day seemed to be a waste of time until a slender, young man with a broad grin and sparkling brown eyes approached him.

"Better shake hands," he announced, the smile still in place. "We're being watched."

The youth's behavior completely baffled the Penetrator, yet something about the handsome young man seemed vaguely familiar. He shook hands with the fellow.

"What do I call you?" the stranger inquired. "I hope you came up with something better than that hokey 'Fred Friendly' name you used before."

Suddenly Mark knew who he was talking to and the reality stunned him. "Bobby? Bobby Reeve?"

"Glad you remember," the other man winked. "Now, what are you calling yourself this week?"

The Penetrator was so startled he almost gave his real name. Bobby Reeve had been a small, bright-eyed kid, just a little boy, when Mark had launched a previous mission in New Orleans against a corrupt fisherman's co-op. Young Bobby had been a gutsy youngster, smart and tough. Mark recalled how ten year old Bobby had recovered from a savage beating and actually killed one of the co-op gangsters in a firefight. Some kind of kid . . . and now he was all grown up. Ten years, the Penetrator thought. *It's been ten years.*

"Uh, call me Jim," he finally answered. "Hell, Bobby . . . I don't know what to say."

"I was sorta shocked to see you, too," Bob admitted with a sheepish grin. "But I didn't have any trouble recognizing you. Haven't changed a bit, *Jim*. Still doing the same old Penetrator stuff, aren't you? Can't keep away from making the headlines, huh?"

"Bob . . ." Mark considered lying to the youth, but then decided it would be unnecessary and an insult to his young friend. "Yes. Same old thing."

"Your secret's safe with me, pal. Has been for a lot of years," Bob assured him, obviously warming to Mark's trust in him.

"I know," the Penetrator replied. Memories flooded back to him. He recalled how fond he'd been of Bobby as a boy, his closeness with the Reeve and the Rubidaux families and Angelique, who had so strongly reminded him of his beloved Donna Morgan. "How's your family, Bob?"

"With twelve brothers and sisters, I'm not sure how everybody's doing myself," the young man answered. "But my father, Gaston, retired from the fishing business and has a nice little shop in Baton Rouge, selling bait and tackle. Uh . . . Angelique got married five years ago."

"I'm glad," Mark replied. He meant it. Angelique had been a painful memory he'd suppressed for the last ten years, but he discovered it no longer hurt to think of her. Time—and Angie Dillon—had healed that old emotional wound. "And what have you been doing with your life?"

"I'm an insurance investigator for Land and Sea Protection," Bob declared with a hint of pride. "When I finished high school, I took a couple years of criminology—and I blame you for influencing me when I was just an impressionable kid and steering me into this racket. I could have joined the police force, but that didn't appeal to me, so I wound up sneaking and peeking for LSP instead."

"What did you mean by that remark that somebody was watching us when we shook hands?" Mark inquired.

"Because we were being watched," Bob confirmed. "Probably still are. You see, when you started asking so many questions about yachts and a crew, one of our clients, LeBeau Yacht Brokers, wondered what you might be up to. Then one of their people remembered seeing you before, all dressed up like a beach bum and hanging around talking to fishermen and wharf rats. They suspected you might be involved in those boat hijackings, so I figured I'd better check you out. Came as quite a surprise to discover you were back in town."

"What do you have on the hijackings, Bob?"

"Figured that's why you were here," the young investigator remarked. "Well, started out old LSP figured this whole pirate business was some sort of insurance fraud scheme. That's when I first got into it. Generally handle the stuff concerning boats since I grew up around them.

"Anyway, turns out this pirate hijacking business is for real. But that still gives us a good reason to investigate. We're the carrier on a lot of brokerages and individual boats. This is going to hurt the sales and renting of yachts. Can't insure something if nobody's willing to buy it. Word about these hijackings is spreading and before long, nobody will want to take the chance of going out into the Gulf and meeting with these pirates. Especially not after what happened to that guy Brockman in the Pacific. I suppose you heard about that."

"Yeah," Mark replied, his voice concealing any personal knowledge of the incident. "Have any leads for me?"

"Hell, I don't have any for myself," Bob sighed. "Hold on. There was one rather peculiar incident happened a while back. I don't see any connection, but if you're involved in this, boatnapping must be bigger than I thought. There's a mercenary recruiter who hangs around the Napoleon House on Rue Royal. One of the other investigators is a Vietnam vet who thinks the job is pretty boring and wants something with a little more action. Goofball actually considered becoming a soldier of fortune. Well, he paid this recruiter a visit, but he decided the guy was full of shit and didn't want anything to do with his outfit."

"So what does this have to do with the stolen boats?" the Penetrator inquired.

"Probably nothing," Bob admitted. "Only the recruiter asked some mighty odd questions. Dave said the guy wanted to know if he suffered from motion sickness or sea sickness."

Mark frowned. "Does seem a little peculiar," he admitted. "But most mercs—at least the type of guys from this country who get involved— tend to be strongly pro-American and anti-communist and highly motivated. They seem to have well-defined principles, and hijacking yachts doesn't look like the sort of activity that would appeal to them. Besides, I've had two encounters with the pirates. They're hoods. Plain old garbage variety street punks, not trained soldiers and damn sure not combat veterans."

"Like I said, I doubt that there's a connection either," Bob repeated. "But this merc recruiter seems like a jerk to Dave. Could be he is involved somehow, or he might know someone who is."

"Guess it's worth checking out," Mark decided. "How do I get in touch with this recruiter?"

"According to Dave, he's easy enough to recognize. The guy wears a black patch over his left eye and there's a scar on that side of his face. Dave also said he spoke with a British accent and he over-did the soldier of fortune image—called himself 'Captain Conway' and he didn't take off his black beret, even when they went upstairs to his office."

"Sounds like I won't have much trouble finding him." Mark glanced at his watch. "If this character's a hood, I'd just as soon pay him a visit before it gets dark. Crooks tend to feel more at home after the sun goes down. Since I'll be meeting him on his turf, I want every edge I can get. How about we meet later this evening and discuss this business in more detail?"

"Sure," Bobby agreed. "Why don't we have dinner at *Le Casier a Homards*? Say, about nine o'clock?"

Mark winced, reminded that no one dined in New Orleans at a sensible hour like five-thirty or six o'clock. "Okay. One thing, Bob," he added. "These pirates are rough customers. Watch out for yourself."

Bobby Reeve smiled. "Don't worry about me," he said, patting a bulge under his left armpit. "I've got a Colt Commander here and I know how to use it. Also carry a High Standard .22 Magnum derringer and a Buck Folding Hunter for back-up." Bob beamed, though he shrugged off the implication. "You know what they say about imitation."

The Penetrator grinned in return. "And I am sincerely flattered. See you at nine."

Mark left his young friend and headed for his rented Mazda, parked beyond the yacht basin. Although pleased to encounter Bobby Reeve again, the fact that the little boy he'd known had now grown into a man contributed to something that had disturbed him since his meeting with Dan Griggs in San Diego. Time had begun to gnaw away at Dan, Professor Haskins, David Red Eagle and, Mark now realized, he, too, had been growing older ... a hazard he'd never even considered until that moment.

9

Hoodlum For Hire

The Penetrator managed to find a parking garage half a block north of Bourbon Street and walked south to the corner of Toulouse and Royal. Across Royal to his right he saw the wrought iron picket fence that surrounded what had once been the Royal Government House, and was now a large museum. Directly ahead, the plastered-over stone walls of a two-story, French Colonial style building, its gray and white trimmed windows covered with iron bars, occupied the corner. A balcony, typical of the French Quarter, protruded on both street sides of the structure, originally constructed as a home in exile for Napoleon Bonaparte, and provided a shelter over the worn sandstone stoop. Dim lights spread yellow fans from inside and the odor of age and stale liquor wafted out in a manner consistent with the establishment's history. The Penetrator crossed Royal and entered.

A scarred old mahogany counter and backbar occupied most of the space in the long, narrow room. A few tables, wrought iron with dingy white marble tops, filled most of the remaining space. The Penetrator crossed to the bar, noting the stained plaster walls, ancient prints and advertisements for Pernod and other French alcoholic beverages, aged cracks and smoke-stained, burnished open wooden beams. Mark approached the bar. A thickly built man with heavy eyelids and a large Gallic nose, asked him what he'd like to drink.

"Right now," Mark replied. "I'm looking for a man. He calls himself Captain Conway."

"That one," the bartender nodded. He obviously made a conscious effort to conceal his distaste for the person Mark had mentioned. "You will find him in the courtyard."

The Penetrator followed the bartender's pointing finger, gave him a dollar for the information and headed for the courtyard.

An interior balcony, with the inevitable wrought iron railing, surrounded the interior garden. Lush, semi-tropical plants, citrus trees and ferns, with huge hanging baskets of philodendron, fuchsia and blooming epiphylum crowded the patrons into isolated islands at tables around the fringe and near the central carved fountain. Mark had to constantly duck and push the swaying containers out of his way while he searched for the merc recruiter. At last he located his man on the far side of the splashing fountain.

At a table, with a brandy snifter and a cup of coffee in front of him, sat Captain Conway. The eyepatch and scar on his cheek left little doubt about his identity. Uncharacteristically, the mercenary recruiter's black beret sat on the table and Mark saw why the man had worn it during his meeting with Bobby's colleague. Tufts of black hair jutted from Conway's head and white marks between the scattered hirsute patches suggested he'd undergone some rather unsuccessful plastic surgery. One scar extended from the forehead to the eyepatch and ended at his left cheek.

The Penetrator watched the man quickly dab his mutilated skull with a handkerchief and hastily don his beret. Although Conway had obviously suffered some sort of fierce injury, probably from a fire, Mark felt no sympathy for him. A sneering smile played at Conway's coarse lips and the single hazel eye seemed to slither to and fro beneath its hooded lid. His nose hooked forward and contributed to his vulture-like appearance. When Mark approached the table, Conway's sly smile slowly expanded.

"Captain Conway?" the Penetrator inquired.

"That's right," the scar-faced merc replied, his voice flavored with an East London accent. "What can I do for you, Mister . . . ?"

"Abbot," Mark supplied. "H. C. Abbot. I hear you're looking for men."

"True," Conway nodded. "A certain type of men to be exact."

"Are you sure this is a good place to talk?" The Penetrator glanced about at the other patrons seated in the courtyard.

"The Napoleon House is a rather appropriate setting for a man in my line of work," Conway stated. "In 1813, Bonapartist supporters among the French population of New Orleans built this house for the deposed Emperor. They hired mercenaries and outfitted them in the Imperial blue-and-white uniforms of the Horse Guard . . ."

"And then they planned to set sail for Europe to free Napoleon, bring him to America and build a new empire," Mark added. "Only by the time they got everything together it was too late. Napoleon had returned to France, lost the Battle of Waterloo and died at St. Helena."

Conway's lone eyebrow rose. "Well, you appear to be a well-read man, Mister Abbot."

"If we're going to discuss history," the Penetrator said dryly. "I suppose we can sit here in the courtyard, but don't you think business should be conducted in a more private atmosphere?"

"Of course," The merc smiled thinly. "Shall we continue this conversation in my, ah, office?"

Conway led Mark through the riot of vegetation to the far end of the courtyard. They mounted a wrought iron staircase to the floor above and walked along the balcony corridor, flanked by closed doors. Conway escorted him to one with the numeral 12 on the top panel and knocked twice.

"Captain Conway," he announced.

The door opened and a man who resembled a fireplug dressed in a cheap brown suit appeared at the threshold. He gazed at Mark with suspicion in his flat, hazel eyes, fixed in a bulldog face.

"Might have a new recruit here, Harry," Conway stated.

"Right, boss," Harry replied in a voice that sounded as though his larynx were wrapped in sandpaper.

Mark realized the "captain's" remark had been unnecessary, which meant it was probably a code phrase—either to let Harry know he could relax or to alert him to possible trouble from their guest.

Conway and the Penetrator entered the room. Instinctively Mark ducked his head, a tall man's reaction to the low ceiling with its richly patinated open beams glowing a deep cordovan hue from age and smoke. The hundred-fifty year old calcinate plaster walls had turned a spiritless gray, streaked here and there with brown water marks and patches missing in spots. The bare, plank floor would have seemed more at home in Colonial Williamsburg, Mark thought. A small roll-top desk had been shoved against one wall and a divan of early nineteen-twenties style occupied another. Three chairs, looking as fully antique as the building, sat at random. A single, bare bulb hung from a braided green-and-yellow cord at the center of the room. A single, narrow window admitted the neon glare of nightlife in the French Quarter.

Harry and another strong-arm type positioned themselves near the door. The other goon was a tall, muscle-bound black man with a shaven head and a Fu-Man Chu mustache. He slapped the door shut with a big palm. His surly expression suggested he'd like to treat Mark's head in a similar manner.

"Who are these guys?" The Penetrator inquired. "Are they both your secretaries or is one of them an accountant?"

The thugs glared at Mark, but Conway waved a hand at them to relax. "Harry and Lou are associates of mine who specialize in dealing with unruly visitors," the merc explained. "Don't let that upset you. They're just here as a precaution and they won't pull your arms out of their sockets unless I tell them to."

"I'm so glad," Mark commented dryly. "What sort of merc outfit are you part of, Captain?"

"The type that makes a lot of money, Mister

Abbot," the one-eyed soldier of fortune assured
him. "Now, tell me something about your combat experience. Vietnam? Rhodesia? Northern
Ireland?"

"Ireland?" Mark raised his eyebrows. "You
mean you'd be willing to hire me if I'd worked
with IRA terrorists?"

"Don't let my British accent worry you,"
Conway laughed. "I am, after all, a man of the
world."

"I spent two tours in Vietnam," the Penetrator
supplied and then added two lies about serving
as a mercenary in the Middle East and South
America. "Now, what sort of deal are you involved in?"

"Well, it's nothing as risky as what you've
already experienced," Conway promised. He sat
at the end of the desk and placed an attaché
case in front of himself. "I am prepared to offer
you five thousand dollars—in advance—and an
additional ten thousand dollars on completion
of the mission."

"One more time," Mark said, trying to restrain his impatience. "What the hell is this
mission about?"

"We all intend to take a nice little cruise down
the Caribbean and pay a visit to one of the
islands there," the merc explained with a smug
smile.

"Which island?" the Penetrator asked. "Cuba?
Haiti? Jamaica?"

"As a matter of fact," Conway admitted, "I
don't know which one it is myself. But it's an
island, not a country and I've been assured that
it will be as easy as killing an old woman in a
wheelchair."

"You know what, Conway?" Mark snapped, adding a cold smile. "I think you're a real asshole and I hope you and your fellow butchers get blown in the weeds the minute you set foot on the shores of this island."

"Really?" Conway's single hazel orb glared at him. "And I think it's time Harry and Lou earned their keep."

Mark pivoted to face the two muscle boys, quickly drawing a Guardfather from his inside suitcoat pocket. Harry and Lou advanced, the fireplug's face expressing grim determination and the black thug grinning with expectation. Both men froze and stared in horrified awe when the Penetrator raised the Guardfather and the long ice-pick blade snapped into place.

Taking advantage of the distraction, Mark immediately kicked Harry between the legs. The ball of his foot crushed into the stocky pug's genitals, causing the hood to wheeze in agony and double over.

"Mutter fuck'a!" Lou exclaimed, his hand plunging inside his sports jacket in search of a pistol.

The Penetrator suddenly shoved Harry into the black hood, throwing Lou off balance. Before the thug could recover and finish drawing his piece, Mark struck again, lancing the tip of the Guardfather into Lou's triceps. The muscle boy screamed as blood spurted from his upper arm to stain the sleeve of his jacket. Mark silenced Lou with a lateral elbow stroke to the facial nerve under the side of his jawbone.

Seeing his bodyguards crumble to the carpet, Conway desperately worked the latches of his briefcase, opened it and reached inside for a

Heckler and Koch P9S 9mm pistol. The Penetrator's arm became a blur and he drew his
MatchMaster to aim it at the startled mercenary's
pale face.

"Give me an excuse, Conway," he invited.

The one-eyed merc slammed his attaché case
shut and shoved it across the desk in surrender.
Harry groaned and began to stir. Mark merely
glanced at him to be certain of his target and
then delivered a fast back kick, catching the
hood in the breast bone with the edge of his
foot. Harry sprawled on his back and gasped for
air like a fish flopping about on the shore.

"What are you, Abbot?" Conway demanded,
holding his arms high. "A cop? Fed? What?"

"I'm a Jehova's Witness," the Penetrator replied grimly. "Guess I'll have to mail you a copy
of *The Watchtower*."

With that, he returned his .45 to its shoulder
leather and left the room.

Captain Roger Conway briefly considered getting his pistol out of the attaché case and following the formidable stranger. But common sense
and a strong sense of self-preservation warned
him not to act on impulse. Gutsy bastard knew
damned good and well he wouldn't try to shoot
it out in the Napoleon House. Instead, Conway
turned his anger on his two stooges.

"You bleedin' idiots!" he snarled, kneeling beside Lou Moore to seize the Guardfather still
jammed in the black man's triceps. Conway savagely yanked the spike weapon from the hood's
arm. Lou moaned loudly and clutched his bloodied limb, rolling on the floor in agony.

"Don't cry on my shoulder, you burr-head

baboon," Conway hissed, tossing the Guardfather aside with contempt. "Or you either, you pee-brained moron!"

"Jesus, boss," Harry McKinnon whined as he painfully rose from the carpet. "How was we supposed to know that fucker'd have a pig-sticker like that?"

"Christ on a crutch!" Conway snapped. "I gave you the code to jump the bastard. Why'd you two wait so long to make your move?"

"Uh . . ." Harry began dully. "Seemed like you wanted to talk to him, boss."

Conway rolled his eyes in frustration. "You imbeciles! I was trying to distract the son of a bitch! Don't you realize who that was? Linsey told us to be on the watch for a great bloody bully-boy who kicks arse like a Bobby in a wog bar. He delivers himself to us like a bleedin' present and you two fuck up like a meeting of Parliament."

"But, boss . . ." Harry gestured helplessly with one hand while the other massaged his battered testicles.

"Oh, shut up!" Conway demanded. "What matters is that this Abbot or whatever he calls himself, is bloody close to finding out what's afoot. That means he'll try another stunt like this again, and soon. This time we'll be ready for him and make certain the snoopin' bastard winds up on a goddamned marble slab."

10

Three For Paradise

A huge red lobster, wearing a napkin and holding a knife and fork in its claws, revolved slowly on the roof of *Le Casier a Homards*. Mark Hardin gazed up at the mechanical crustacean and fleetingly entertained the whimsical and rather macabre notion that it would be ironic if the restaurant proved to be infested with giant lobsters who dined on unsuspecting humans, lured into the place by its colorful sign, unaware that it presented an image of exactly what lurked within.

Fortunately, his sci-fi daydream didn't materialize when he entered *Le Casier a Homards*. Instead, a perfectly human *maitre d'*, dressed in a tuxedo asked if he'd made a reservation. When Mark explained that Mister Robert Reeve had arranged for a table, the *maitre d'* glanced over a list mounted on a lectern that looked like it should have been in front of the altar of a church.

"*Oui*," the man announced. "*Monsieur* Reeve, party of four."

The number of people surprised the Penetrator, but he allowed himself to be escorted to the dining room where he found Bobby seated at a table with two exceptionally lovely young girls.

The females offered him twin dazzling smiles and Bobby grinned in his familiar impish manner that hadn't changed since he was ten years old.

"Glad you could make it, Jim," he announced, obviously pleased by the confused expression on Mark's face. "How do you like the company I provided?"

"Quite a surprise," the Penetrator answered, wondering what the hell Bobby thought he was doing. They were supposed to be discussing the boat hijackings, not double-dating with a pair of sweet young things. Or could they be a couple of the high-priced hookers for which the Quarter had become justly famous?

"Sharon Fay." Bob gestured toward the auburn-haired beauty seated to Mark's right. She had large gray-green eyes and a wide mouth that made the Penetrator think about oral sex, especially when she smiled at him and raised an eyebrow in an openly suggestive manner.

"And this is Cindy Brown," Bob continued, referring to the other girl, an equally gorgeous honey blonde, with a smooth oval face and a turned up nose. However, Cindy proved even more bold than her dark-haired counterpart, sliding the tip of her tongue along her upper lip when Mark turned to face her.

"Well, girls," Bob said, clearly having a ball at the expense of a bewildered Penetrator. "How do you like Jim so far?"

"So far," Sharon repeated, leaning forward to display a generous view of cleavage. "So good."

"Very good," Cindy added, plucking an olive on a skewer from her martini and slowly licking it.

"The girls are going to take a trip down the coast of Mexico to Yucatan," Bob explained. "They have a first-rate thirty-eight foot Grandbanks Trawler—insured by Land and Sea Protection, naturally—but they need a nice, healthy he-man to crew for them. Since I can't get away from the office and my fiance would kill me, I decided you'd be the next best choice, Jim."

"How considerate," Mark replied, still trying to deal with the curve Bobby had thrown him.

As the title of the restaurant suggested, lobster proved to be the house specialty. They all selected their choice from a tankful of live crustaceans and returned to their seats for a round of martinis. The girls chatted away about their life in a college dormitory, making it sound as though they'd been locked into a convent against their will. Bobby talked about his investigations and told a few jokes and Mark tried to hold his own in the conversation without seeming dull, commenting about sailing and what Mexico looked like that time of year.

The Penetrator didn't have to do much to be the center of the girls' attention. Cindy placed a hand to her cheek and announced that she'd dropped her napkin. Mark bent over to pick it up and saw Cindy purposely pull her skirt up to show off plenty of shapely, pantyhose-encased leg. A few minutes later, Sharon repeated the napkin-dropping routine.

Mark dutifully retrieved it and noticed that the auburn-haired girl was slightly more subtle than Cindy. Sharon had already hiked up her skirt before she got clumsy and the hemline rode high enough on her thighs for Mark to get a glimpse of yellow panties.

When the girls finally decided to visit the ladies room, leaving together as women always do, the Penetrator glared at a thoroughly amused Bobby Reeve.

"Bobby, what do you think you're doing?" he demanded.

"Getting a raging hard-on over those two," Bob replied. "And don't tell me you aren't feeling the same way. Jesus, are you going to have *some kind* of trip with those honeys."

"Don't you realize you're exposing those girls to a helluva lot of potential danger?" Mark snapped.

"Gee, and I figured you'd go easy on them . . ."

"Damnit, Bobby!"

"Hold on, Jim," Bobby insisted. "I tried to talk Cindy and Sharon out of making that cruise, but they're not taking this pirate business serious and insist on exposing themselves . . ." he began to giggle and covered it with a long sip from his martini. "To danger, that is."

"I don't like it," Mark objected with a frown.

"Hey, whether you go with those two co-ed nymphos or not, they still intend to make the voyage to Yucatan," Bobby told him. "Either way, with the girls on board, that Grandbanks Trawler is going to be a ripe target for the pirates."

"Bait?" Mark glared at Bobby.

"Look," Bobby sighed. "If anyone is using those girls to bait the hijackers, it's themselves. We can only supply them with the best protection possible—you."

The Penetrator realized Bob Reeve had a point. If the hijackers did attack the girls' boat, he might finally get an opportunity to capture one

of the pirates and get a few answers. Instead of
a steady increase of questions and corpses.

Naturally, being a healthy young man with a
normal sex drive, Mark couldn't help thinking
about Cindy and Sharon's suggestive expressions,
the ample views of cleavage and the cheesecake
show they'd displayed under the table. From
New Orleans to Yucatan with a pair of beautiful,
sex-hungry girls like those . . .

"For the sake of the mission," he declared,
managing to keep a straight face. "I'll do it."

Mark Hardin and the girls set out in the *Isis*,
their Grandbanks Trawler, the following morning. Cindy and Sharon seemed to have decided
to have a contest to see who could wear the
skimpiest halter top and the briefest, tightest-
fitting pair of shorts. If the Penetrator had been
asked to judge, he would have called it a tie.

When it came time for the tricky task of navi-
gating down the Mississippi Delta, he found himself wishing the girls had a little nautical knowledge to go along with their gorgeous bodies
and lustful attitudes. The *Isis* was blessed by
favorable weather—a clear, blue sky, with only
a hint of puffy white cirrus clouds and no chop
on the river. Under motor power until they
cleared the main shipping channel, the first three
hours of the cruise went smoothly enough.

Then Mark spotted what appeared to be a
tiny black island in their way. He recognized it
as a cypress knee. The Penetrator spun the wheel
to the right to avoid contact with the stubborn
relic of a tree. He made only a point on the port
beam and the wheel refused to turn farther.

"One of you girls raise the halyard," he

commanded, feverishly fighting the wheel. It was no use. Something had gone wrong with the rudder. "The other get to the backstays and raise the lift."

"Halyard?" Sharon inquired, thoroughly confused.

"Backstays?" Cindy's voice sounded equally baffled.

The Penetrator tried to judge the distance from the boat to the gnarled hump of cypress that jutted above the surface of the water like the head of a waiting sea monster. It seemed eager to dash the *Isis* into white kindling and shredded canvas. Fifty yards . . . seventy-five at the most, he decided.

"We have to get those sails up fast," Mark declared.

"But we're under motor power," Cindy protested.

"Sharon," Mark ordered, having decided she was the brighter of the pair. "Take the wheel and turn it this way," he gave her a demonstration. "And hold it. She won't answer to the helm and we need the sail's sideward kick to clear that thing."

The girl moved toward the stern and took the wheel. "You mean *toward* that thing out there?" She stared in horror at the cypress, suddenly aware of the danger they were in.

"That's how you steer a sailboat," the Penetrator explained curtly. "Just the opposite from a car."

He galloped aft and rapidly untied the square knots of the sheets attached to the halyard. The line went slack and he quickly hauled on it, raising the lift and the main sail to catch the wind. The speed of the trawler increased dramatically from ten knots to almost seventeen. Sideward pressure on the lift boom slowly nosed the bow around.

Mark held his breath while the boat sped past the obstruction, praying its hull wouldn't connect with the stony knees that extended underwater. Under other circumstances, the Penetrator would have appreciated the natural beauty of the ancient, tidewater hardened remnant of a once grand tree, instead of regarding it as a deadly, rock-hard adversary.

"Hey," Cindy remarked, gazing over the starboard tack rail at the cypress. "Aren't we kinda close to this thing?"

"Yeah," Mark replied through clenched teeth, expecting to hear the ugly grating sound of the keel striking the submerged knees, followed by the ominous crunch of breaking wood.

Regardless of his misgivings, the *Isis* missed the sunken bole by more than a foot. The Penetrator and his female companions sighed with relief after they'd left it behind.

Once out of the Mississippi seaway and certain that the ocean would be calm for a while and no other hazards were in sight, Mark killed the engine and, with the girls inexpert help, hoisted all sail. Then he stripped down to his swimming trunks and donned a Kai Dive Mask before he headed aft and climbed over the stern of the trawler to hop into the ocean. Inspecting the rudder, he soon discovered the cause of its malfunction—a discarded length of fishnetting had somehow gotten fouled around it. After removing the obstruction, he climbed back on board and announced his "heroic efforts" at mak-

ing "repairs" to the girls. Sharon and Cindy gazed
at his lean, muscular body with open admira-
tion and Mark wondered which one would be
better in bed.

The rest of the day proved pleasantly uneventful
ful and the trio relaxed and enjoyed the trip.
The girls changed to skimpy bikinis and placed
beach towels on the foredeck to lie in the sun.
Mark set the auto-pilot and tried to concentrate
on fishing. He reminded himself that the pirates
could well be lurking somewhere in the distance.
Still, Cindy and Sharon were terrible distrac-
tions— and worse, he began to wonder if they
weren't a pair of teases.

Well, he thought. Sex wasn't everything. It's
only more fun than anything else.

They dined on broiled baracuda Mark caught,
diced palm hearts from the canned goods locker
and chilled white wine. By nightfall, both girls
had retired to the cabins below the spar deck
and the Penetrator morosely decided their nym-
pho-act was a come-on with a let-down. He took
the evening sighting with the sextant, logged
progress on the chart and corrected course, checking the drift compensator and leaving conning
the boat to the auto-pilot. When he returned to
New Orleans, he'd be tempted to give Bobby
Reeve a good hard kick in the rear for getting
him stuck in such a situation. Sailing to Mexico
with two luscious girls who'd both locked the lids
to their cookie jars left him feeling less than
grateful.

Mark mentally scolded himself for his somewhat immature, if totally human, notions. He
was, after all, on a mission and frolicking with a
pair of college co-eds could hardly be consid-

ered a crucial part of it. He'd brought aboard an aluminum suitcase full of weapons selected for the cruise and, although he knew everything was in perfect working order, it never hurt to check. He headed for his cuddy to inspect his equipment and hopefully get his mind off Sharon and Cindy.

The Penetrator opened the door of his cabin and discovered Sharon Fay waiting for him. She sat on his bunk, her shapely, trim legs crossed, beautifully displayed by the hip-high hemline of a black lace nightie. Her perfectly formed breasts swelled against the flimsy fabric, erect nipples jutting forward like a pair of brass studs from large, dark areolas.

"Cindy and I cut cards to decide who gets to sleep with you first," Sharon explained. "Of course, if you want to make it with her tonight . . ."

"I don't see anything wrong with the present accomodations," Mark assured her with a great deal more calm than he felt. He closed and latched the door.

Soon they were riding into a private paradise together. . . .

11

Murder In Paradise

No science fiction or fantasy writer can match the uncanny wonders of reality and some of the most incredible phenomena of nature are to be found in the sea. Mark Hardin and the girls stared in spellbound amazement as four flying fish broke the surface of the water to glide several feet before diving back into the waves. It was a bizarre and startling spectacle to watch the winged fish literally sailing through the air, no matter how many times it had been viewed before.

"Do you think there might be something to those Loch Ness Monster stories?" Sharon inquired. She leaned close to Mark, tracing her fingernails along his bare chest.

"Could be," the Penetrator replied, turning his attention from the flying fish to another sight of natural splendor, thanks to the low neckline of Sharon's tank top.

"Giant squid turned out to be more than an old fisherman's horror story. A number of animal species have remained unchanged by evolution since the time of the dinosaurs. Giant eel larva have been discovered that are ten times larger than normal—which could mean the adults might be almost sixty feet long. I'd say it's possible there's some truth behind the legend of Nessy and other sea serpent stories," he grinned. "But I wouldn't worry about encountering one of them on this cruise."

"I don't know about that," Cindy declared. She pressed her firm, lithe body, clad in a white halter top and brief, tight shorts, against his naked upper torso. "We've found a delightfully big serpent at sea. Haven't we, Sharon?"

Mark felt Cindy's hands probe his crotch. She carefully opened his fly and knelt before him. Cindy's lips slipped over his aroused maleness, slowly taking the length of his fleshy shaft in her mouth. Mark had a fleeting thought of gratitude for the continued excellent functioning of the auto-pilot.

Sharon began to kiss and nip at his neck and shoulders while Cindy's head moved back and forth, her lips and tongue expertly stroking him. Then Sharon perched herself on the taffrail and took Mark's face in her hands, turning it toward her now bare breasts. He opened his mouth and drew on a stiff nipple, gently teasing it with teeth and tongue, while his fingers drew down the top of her short-shorts and strolled teasingly through the whispy strands of pubic hair that covered her swollen, moist-hot mound.

These girls are going to wear me out, the Penetrator thought.

Either Cindy or Sharon or both of them together had been constantly calling on Mark for sexual services—in their cabins, in his, on deck and on the galley floor. He wouldn't be surprised if they next suggested trying to do it in the ocean. Jesus, he thought, he'd have to eat clam chowder for a month and take vitamin E injections to recover from this trip.

Although the sexual banquet and the natural beauty of sailing down the Gulf of Mexico made the cruise exquisitely pleasurable, two things still nagged at the Penetrator. He felt occasional pangs of guilt for his behavior with the girls. Mark had been thinking of retiring from the "Penetrating" business and marrying Angie Dillon. Yet now he was on board a yacht—not unlike the type he'd planned to buy for Angie and the twins—"penetrating" Sharon and Cindy morning, afternoon and all night long. The conservative, conventional, part of Mark's mind told him that this put him in the category of all-time bastards.

The second matter that flawed an otherwise perfect arrangement was the fact the hijackers were still at large and could strike at any moment.

Then the fire in Mark's loins became too great to allow thoughts of anything else. He exploded in Cindy's mouth and she greedily drank him. The girls quickly slipped out of their skimpy outfits and Mark followed their example. The trio headed for a beach blanket on the deck and the Penetrator hoped his stamina would see him through the voyage—and that the pirates wouldn't arrive for at least another hour or two.

A distant squall raced along the horizon, trailing wispy gray sheets of rain on the third afternoon out. Cindy stood on top of the cabinhouse, legs wide apart, one arm wrapped around the mast, watching it while the wind blew her long blonde hair into a wild tangle. She was buck-naked. A sudden frown creased her brow and she peered intently toward the southeast.

"Hey, Jim!" she called down to the Penetrator. "There's a sail over there. Another boat, coming this way."

Mark Hardin, standing at the wheel in the cockpit, snapped on the auto-pilot and lifted a pair of Bushnell 8×30 binoculars and examined the boat. The vessel, a Newport ketch, seemed familiar, even before it drew close enough for him to read the hastily painted-out legend on the bow—*All American*.

He lowered the glasses and turned to face Sharon, motioning for Cindy to come down. They stared at him, surprised and more than a little frightened by the hard line of his mouth and the savage fury expressed in his dark, smoldering eyes.

"We're about to get into one hell of a firefight," he grimly announced.

"Come on, Jim," Cindy urged. "That isn't funny . . ."

"He isn't joking," Sharon told her in a hard, flat voice.

"Ahoy, trawler!" an amplified voice called to them from a bullhorn on the *All American*. "We need assistance. Request we come alongside and board your vessel to use the radio."

The Penetrator expected the distress call and had already gotten out a megaphone to reply to it. "Permission granted," his voice boomed in response. "We'll be glad to receive your party."

He lowered the bullhorn. A cold, murderous smile crept across his face. The Penetrator would arrange one hell of a reception for the hijackers.

"Come on," he said sharply. "You girls are going down to your cabins until this is over. When the shooting starts, I want you below the waterline."

"Shooting?" Cindy gasped. "Hey, wait a minute . . ."

"Shut up, Cindy," Sharon commanded. "Looks like those pirate stories are for real."

"As real as death," Mark replied, leading the way to the cabins. "Do either of you know how to use a gun?"

"Of course we don't!" Cindy exclaimed indignantly.

"Speak for yourself," Sharon snapped. "Bobby told us you were some sort of federal cop. You got a spare piece for me?"

Mark looked at Sharon Fay, impressed by her response. He hadn't expected such courage and cool-headed efficiency from either of the girls. The Penetrator led them to his cuddy, tossed his aluminum suitcase on the bunk and unlocked it. "Figure you can handle a Star PD?" he asked Sharon.

"That's a forty-five cal built sort of like a Colt Commander isn't it?" Sharon replied, revealing that her attitude was founded on solid firearms knowledge.

"Honey, you got it," he enthused, opening the suitcase to extract a pistol and two spare magazines. He handed them to Sharon and watched her calmly jack a round into the chamber and flick on the safety catch.

She looked on as Mark removed a strange-looking weapon that resembled a fat, eighteen-inch tube with a pistol grip and trigger mechanism welded on. The gun baffled her for a moment, although her entire family back in Vermont were firearms enthusiasts and she had handled quite an assortment of weapons personally and had a Life Membership in the National Rifle Association. Suddenly Sharon realized what Jim Banner's gun must be.

"That's a Sid McQueen Sidewinder submachine gun, isn't it?"

Mark blinked. "You're just full of surprises, Sharon," he commented, busily strapping on a web belt that contained magazine pouches and a holster for his Safari Arms MatchMaster.

"I read a description of the Sidewinder in a novel about this mercenary operation in Libya . . ." she offered, then frowned. "Or was it El Salvador?"

"Look, you and Cindy go lock yourselves in a cuddy," he instructed briskly. "And don't come out until I tell you to, okay?"

"Are you two insane?" Cindy squeaked in a wondering tone. "All these awful guns and talk of killing. The only thing to do is co-operate, do what they want and it will be all right. So what if they take the boat? It's insured. But you . . . you . . ."

Sudden disgust washed over the Penetrator's face. "These scumbags wasted a friend of mine not long ago and did their damnedest to do me in. I'd rather 'be nice' to a shark." He turned to Sharon. "Get her down to a cabin and keep her there."

Sharon dragged the still-protesting Cindy away while the Penetrator added two M-34 incendiary-fragmentation grenades to his arsenal and quickly saw to the girls' safety. After he was certain they were both locked in Sharon's cuddy, he headed toward the gangway to the cabin section and waited at the foot of the ladder for the *All American* to arrive.

The private vessel had already closed the distance between itself and the other vessel. Mark saw the bowsprit of the Newport ketch glide past the cockpit of the *Isis*. The trawler suddenly trembled through her timbers when the hijackers' craft bumped against the hull without the aid of fenders.

"Something's wrong," Joe Linsey declared. He stood at the bow of the *All American* and suspiciously gazed over the deserted decks of the *Isis*. "Why are they hiding?"

Captain Roger Conway stepped over beside Linsey. "And who was the man that replied to our distress call?" the mercenary demanded. "I thought you said there were only supposed to be a couple of birds on board this thing?"

Voices travel dramatically across water and Mark heard the men converse, instantly recognizing Conway's East London accent. So there *was* a connection between the pirates and the mercenary recruiter. Did that mean the hijackings were somehow associated with the invasion of a Caribbean island Conway mentioned?

"Sam, Pete, Tom!" Linsey commanded. "Hop on board and check the tub out. Watch your step. This could be some sort of trick."

The sound of booted feet landing heavily on the deck confirmed that the order had been obeyed. Aware that the pirates could easily guess his position—outside the deckhouse there wasn't much cover available on the *Isis*—Mark decided the only edge in his favor was the Sid McQueen model music box. The pirates clearly expected trouble, but could he give them more than they were prepared to deal with?

He knew only one way to find out.

Mark suddenly broke cover and confronted the three startled gunmen who'd boarded the *Isis*. The trio of hoods were armed with short barreled pistols. None of them thought that taking a boat at sea would be much of a challenge—and they certainly hadn't planned on taking on somebody armed with a submachine gun.

The Penetrator gambled that the invaders wouldn't start shooting immediately. He proved to be right. They hesitated for less than a second, but long enough for Mark to open fire on the trio.

The Sidewinder snarled like a mechanical hound at the Gates of Hell, spitting death and damnation. Only God knows about the former, but three .45 caliber projectiles certainly delivered the latter condition to Samuel Curtis. The hoodlum's heart and lungs got instantly chopped into diced-organ hash and a criminal career that had started fifteen years before as a junior mugger who specialized in swiping purses from little old ladies, ended abruptly at the hand of a tough, determined young man.

Curtis' corpse catapulted backward by the force of the heavy slugs and collided with Tom Rich. A scrawny man with a round little pot-belly and a thinning hairline, Rich couldn't have cared less about Curtis's plight. He had enough problems of his own, courtesy of two Sidewinder rounds in the face.

One semi-jacketed hollow point missile struck Rich in his receding chin, shattering the jawbone. Blood-stained teeth spewed between his lips like a mouthful of ivory marbles. The other bullet had punctured the left lens of Rich's thick glasses and drilled a vicious hole under his eyebrow next to the bridge of his nose. Rich's eyeball popped out of its cracked socket to be impaled by the jagged shards of glass that remained in the rim of his spectacles. The middle-aged thug fired his snub-nosed .357 Magnum into the deck planking and he crumpled in a senseless, quivering heap. If a good brain surgeon had been available, Tom Rich might have survived to spend the rest of his life as a human vegetable.

The third pirate, Pete Woodley, had been fortunate enough to be out of the direct line of the Penetrator's fire, and close enough to the spar deck to leap for cover. The young, tow-headed hood cowered behind his shelter, well aware that his Charter Arms .38 revolver was no match for a submachine gun.

Since the *All American* and the *Isis* still drifted close enough to occasionally touch hulls, Joe Linsey and Roger Conway got a good look at the wrathful figure who cut down two of their men in a shred of a second. Conway's mouth dropped open when he recognized the man he knew as H. C. Abbot.

"It's him!" the mercenary cried.

Linsey's astonishment was even greater than Conway's. "Holy fuck!" he exclaimed, stunned when he saw the face of a man he'd believed to have been killed twelve years ago in Saigon. "That's Mark Hardin!"

Before either man could say or do anything else, the muzzle of the Sidewinder swung toward them. Linsey and Conway hit the deck—literally—as a three-round burst of .45 projectiles smacked into the wooden spar above their heads.

The Penetrator had intentionally aimed high, wanting to pin down Conway and the bearded pirate commander. They obviously ranked higher among the hijackers than the cannon fodder he'd just sent to the Big Thug Hang-Out in the Sky. That meant they'd be apt to know more details about the operation than the lesser goons and Mark wanted at least one of them alive to play twenty questions with.

However, he couldn't ignore the safety of the girls either, so he had to take out the third gunman still on board the *Isis*. After forcing Linsey and Conway to duck, Mark swiftly charged forward and executed a fast shoulder roll. His body came to rest against the bulkhead, the Sidewinder pointed directly at the position Pete Woodley had fled to.

"Shit," the Penetrator hissed. The scumbag was gone. He must have climbed from the bow toward the stern and circled around to the opposite side of the spar deck.

Mark ventured a peek between the top of the port bulwark and the rail to see if the two creep commanders were still hugging the deck of the *All American*. He didn't like what he saw. Two more figures appeared on the hijackers' yacht. The Penetrator hadn't whittled down the odds quite as much as he'd hoped—and the pirates proved to be better armed than he'd expected.

Bruno, the giant mute killer, and a chunky

black guy named Ronald Bezzler, had unpacked some special gear that had been stocked in case a firefight with the Coast Guard occurred. Both men aimed M-16 assault rifles at Mark's position and opened fire with the selector switches on full-auto.

Fortunately for the Penetrator, both Bruno and Bezzler were about as skilled with firearms as a hippopotamus is with a pair of knitting needles. The silent hulk had never had much interest in guns and he preferred to kill with his bare hands. Bruno had once been a "pick-up fighter" who worked with a has-been boxer turned promoter by arranging for matches with New Orleans stevedores willing to face Bruno in brutal dockyard brawls.

At the conclusion of one such fight, Bruno pinned an already-unconscious opponent and attempted to hammer the man's skull apart with his fists. Half a dozen stevedores came to the victim's rescue. Bruno managed to take out three of them before being knocked down and savagely stomped. His larnyx had been crushed in the process and whatever notions of humanity he may have had before were lost with his voice.

Bezzler, on the other hand, had missed an opportunity to receive military training in firearms because he'd been granted a General Discharge from the U.S. Marine Corps before he could complete boot camp, being deemed mentally unfit for the service.

Since he'd joined the hijackers, the idea of being a pirate had become a fetish with Bezzler. He'd taken to wearing a polka dot neckerchief around his head and a big gold ring in his right ear lobe. Two thirds of his body had been decorated with tatoos and he occasionally carried a dull-edged cutlass in a red sash bound around his thick waist.

Bezzler once offered Roger Conway fifty dollars for his eyepatch, to which the mercenary asked him if he'd like to have need of one permanently. On another occasion, he'd tried to convice Linsey to hoist the Jolly Roger during the hijackings. He was told if he ever brought a skull-and-crossbones flag on board, they'd find some way to make him walk the plank.

The M-16s rattled out copper-jacketed 5.56 mm slugs until the twenty round magazines of both weapons had been exhausted. Bruno grunted and fumbled with the magazine catch of his rifle. Bezzler shook his M-16, not quite certain why it quit working. Joe Linsey watched him try to fire the empty weapon and shake it a second time, and cursed himself for "hiring that crazy nigger" in the first place.

Mark Hardin remained unharmed, still sprawled behind the cover of the bulwark. The inept marksmanship of the hijackers amazed him. A hail of 5.56mm bullets had struck the spar deck, chewed into the mast and splintered the taffrail. Only a few had hit close to his position. Suspecting some sort of trick—although having no idea what it might be—he decided to pull an explosive rabbit out of his figurative hat.

The Penetrator pulled the pin of an M-34 and hurled it over the top rail. The grenade fuse detonated the explosive four seconds later. A terrific blast erupted at the stern of the *All American*. Chunks of ragged wood and twisted metal were blown in all directions. Some of the debris landed on the decks of the *Isis*—including an ornamental cutlass short sword and a gold earring with a shred of ebony flesh still attached.

Although he'd tried to protect his hearing, Mark's ears were still ringing when he glanced over the side to see the thermite-frag charge of the M-34 had not only turned the stern of the *All American* into a pile of splinters, it had ignited a fierce fire that rapidly danced across the length of the pirate vessel. A man's voice shouted something and then Mark heard a dull buzzing sound that seemed far away. Suddenly a red-and-yellow speedboat appeared in the distance. The tiny craft threw a high rooster tail of water behind it, rapidly dwindling in size as it retreated from the disabled yacht. He recognized the three passengers of the speedboat—a powerful giant, a man with a black beret and a bearded figure at the wheel.

The Penetrator rose to his feet and fired a few hopeless rounds at the fleeing speedster. Then he watched the escaping pirates cut across the water at 40 knots. The hijackers, or at least the pair he'd wanted to capture, had eluded him and all he had accomplished had been to rid the world of three more pieces of human filth and the destruction of a yacht Clell Brockman had meant to deliver to a former Dallas football player.

Two pistol shots cracked, followed by the bellow of a heavier caliber weapon. Mark realized he'd left one of the original three pirate invaders unaccounted for—with Sharon and Cindy still in a cabin below deck.

He dashed to the spar deck and quickly descended the ladder to the companionway, Sidewinder held ready.

Mark didn't need it.

Pete Woodley's body lay sprawled in the companionway in front of Sharon's cabin. Blood stained his shirt front, revealing where two .45 caliber slugs had crashed into his body.

"Sharon! Cindy!" Mark shouted as he gazed at the cabin door. Two large holes in the wooden slats explained how Woodley had received the bullets in his chest. A pair of smaller holes near the doorknob suggested the hoodlum had used the .38 that lay beside his corpse.

The door creaked open and Sharon Fay's tear-stained face looked up at the Penetrator. She still held the Star PD firmly in both hands. Mark assured her everything was over now and gently relieved the girl of the pistol.

"He tried to ... to force ... his way in ..." Sharon began, half sobbing. "I told ... Cindy ... to stay away from ... from the door ... but she ..."

Mark took the girl into his arms. She buried her face against his chest and wept. The Penetrator saw Cindy Brown's lovely body, lying on the floor of the cuddy within. Cindy's lifeless eyes stared up at the ceiling, her sensuous mouth now twisted into a frozen expression of pain and horror. Mark cursed himself for allowing one of the pirates to slip past him during the firefight with the crew of the *All American*. His lip curled downward in a bitter expression and he promised every man involved in the hijacking business would pay for destroying a harmless young girl.

"He . . . he tried to shoot the lock . . ." Sharon whimpered, clinging to Mark for comfort. "And Cindy . . . got hit by . . . by the bullets . . ."

"Take it easy, hon," the Penetrator urged.

"Then I shot through the door." Sharon's voice suddenly became firm, with a trace of satisfaction in her tone. "And I killed the bastard.

12

"Knock, Knock"

"Excuse me, Ma'am," the Penetrator began, addressing the desk clerk-switchboard operator of the Callicutt Hotel. "But could you tell me Roger Conway's room number?"

The woman behind the desk, a strikingly lovely lady in her early thirties, raised her narrow eyebrows. A nametag labeled her as JAN. "You're a friend of Captain Conway's?" she asked, obviously finding an affirmative answer difficult to believe.

"Not exactly." Mark shrugged. "I'm here to help him move some furniture. He's going to be moving out soon, you know."

"Really?" a smile played at Jan's expressive full mouth. "That is, the Captain didn't mention it."

"He's a bit close-mouthed at times," the Penetrator offered.

Jan rolled her swivel chair over to a list of tenant's room numbers. Mark studied her legs with appreciation while she looked for Conway's residence.

"Room twenty-three," Jan announced.

"Thanks." The Penetrator turned to leave, then

added, "Oh, this furniture we'll be moving is sort of heavy so we might make something of a racket. If any of the other tenants complain about the noise, just tell them it's okay and we won't be long getting everything finished. Fair enough?"

"Sure," Jan nodded.

Mark Hardin stepped into the elevator and pressed a button for the second floor. He briefly recalled the events of the last two days. After delivering Sharon to safety at Merida, Yucatan, he'd flown back to New Orleans and reported the bad news about the cruise to Bobby Reeve. The young insurance investigator had been surprised to hear that Captain Conway had been one of the hijackers because his sources claimed the merc recruiter was still doing business at the Napoleon House.

When he heard this, the Penetrator asked Bobby to keep a lid on everything until he could have a "chat" with Conway. Bobby's reply consisted of a single question, "You want some company?" Mark declined and assured Bobby he'd pay him another visit before he left New Orleans, although he felt certain, as he walked out of Bobby's office, he'd never see his young friend again.

The elevator doors opened with an electric hum and the Penetrator stepped into a long hallway with doors along both sides. He located the one with 23 on its top panel and glanced about to be certain no one watched before he knocked on the door.

"It's me, Harry," Mark rasped hoarsely, recalling the gravely voice of one of the thugs he'd encountered at the Napoleon House.

The door opened and Roger Conway's ugly,

one-eyed face appeared. Mark slammed his fist into it as hard as he could.

Propelled by the punch, Conway staggered backward into his handsomely furnished living-room. The Penetrator followed, delivering a fast left hook to the mercenary recruiter's jaw. Conway stumbled into a coffe table and fell over it, knocking a hand-carved chess set to the floor. The merc tried to rise, but Mark chopped the side of his hand into Conway's mastoid behind his left ear. The recruiter of corruption crashed to the carpet and laid still.

"Not as noisy as I figured it'd be," Mark muttered. He closed the front door and approached Conway's prone figure, reaching into a pocket for a pair of plastic riot cuffs.

Without warning, the merc's arms lashed out, sweeping one of Mark's feet out from under him. The Penetrator hopped backward, trying to keep his balance, and fell against a television set mounted on a lightweight aluminum bookcase. The TV tipped forward, taking the case with it. It made a resounding crash, punctuated by the implosion of the tube.

Mark's attention remained on Conway.

The merc had scrambled from the floor and dashed to a small end table by the couch. He yanked open a drawer and darted a hand to-ward it to grab his H&K P9S pistol. The Pene-trator's foot stamped on the drawer, slamming it and nearly catching Conway's fingers in the process.

The back of Mark's fist swung into the merc's face, striking him in the center of an already-broken nose. Conway cried out and fell onto the couch. His arms shot overhead to seize a lamp from another end table. The Penetrator saw the action in time to dodge the light fixture when Conway threw it. Conway's missile sailed across the room and connected with a $2,000 Sony stereo set. Neither man paid attention to the shatter of glass and porcelain or the agonized shriek of what had been a Brahms concerto.

Mark had to give the mercenary credit. The guy was a lot tougher than he looked. Conway had managed to bolt to a closet next to the kitchenette, hoping to get his hands on a 12 ga. Winchester pump shotgun stored there. The Penetrator leaped forward like a vengeful leopard, pouncing on Conway's back. Both men fell against the closet door.

Holding the back of Conway's collar with one hand, Mark drove a karate *seiken* into the merc's left kidney. The one-eyed man groaned. The Penetrator then swiftly slipped his arm under Conway's to apply a half-nelson and promptly smashed the guy's forehead into the doorjam.

Releasing his victim with one hand, Mark kept the other arm hooked under Conway's armpit as he stepped forward, pivoted and bent slightly at the knees.

The mercenary whirled over the Penetrator's hip in a variation of an *osotagari* throw. Conway crashed into a small kitchen table and two plastic-backed chairs. Mark gazed down at the mercenary, who lay amid the wreckage of furniture. The Penetrator cautiously pulled Conway's arms behind his back and cuffed his wrists together.

Barely conscious, the man didn't offer any further resistance.

Breathing rather hard, Mark walked to the

refrigerator, opened the door and found an open bottle of Gallo red wine. It'll do, he thought, taking the green bottle. He poured its contents over Conway's head. The mercenary groaned loudly and glared up at his captor. Blood oozed from his mouth and nostrils and dark bruises decorated his homely face.

"Okay," the Penetrator began, drawing a Guardfather from the inside pocket of his suit jacket. "I've had enough exercise for one day. Talk!"

The spike-like blade of the Guardfather snapped into view. Conway swallowed hard. "Go fuck yourself."

Mark smiled. "Have it your way, fella. You either tell me about the hijackings or I jam this thing up your nose," he declared, bending quickly to thrust the point of his Guardfather under Conway's right nostril.

"What do you want to know about them?" the merc asked, wisely deciding to forget about bravado.

"Who are you working for?"

"Colonel Treavor Jacoby."

"I've heard of him," Mark replied. "Commander of one of the most unprincipled merc armies in the business. Most of the men I've been coming up against are street hoods, not trained soldiers. Who else is involved?"

"My contact is a man named Joe Linsey," Conway answered. "You saw him on the boat the other day."

"Where do I find him?"

"If I knew, I'd bloody well tell you," the merc said angrily. "The bastard sent me back here to tie up loose ends and see to it the men all lie

low and wait to be contacted. We're all going to
be taken to some place in the Caribbean where
some lunatic plans to set up a paradise for
gangsters."

"Where?"

"I don't know."

"You're about to get the worst case of nasal
congestion in history," the Penetrator sighed,
inserting the point of his Guardfather inside
Conway's nostril.

"Christ" the merc insisted. "It's the truth. None
of us were told any more than we had to know.
Jacoby just told me to try to recruit more men
for the strike force to invade a goddamned island.
After they get their bleedin' conquest, then all of
us here in the States would be called in to help
run things and we'd all get a bloody great piece
of the action."

"Why hijack the boats?"

"What were we supposed to do? Steal a goddamned Naval Destroyer? Had to get some way
to sail in and invade the island that wouldn't
seem suspicious. Who'd think a bunch of pretty
white yachts would be carrying an army of
mercenaries, eh?"

"Yeah," Mark said dryly.

"Look, Hardin," Conway began. "Let's make
a deal . . ."

The Penetrator stiffened. "How do you know
my name?"

Conway saw the hardness in his captor's eyes
and swallowed nervously. "Linsey mentioned it.
He recognized you on the boat. Didn't say how
he knew you, just that he figured you'd been
dead for the last twelve years."

"Too bad he told you that, Captain," Mark sighed.

Then he drove the Guardfather into Conway's nostril.

The blade quickly entered the nasal passage and pierced through into the merc's brain, killing him instantly.

The Penetrator rose and shook his head, feeling his stomach knot. Killing a man in self-defense was one thing, but he could never get used to executing one in cold blood. Still, he'd had no other choice if he intended to keep his identity a secret—and to do otherwise would be signing his own death warrant. Roger Conway had been a criminal with plenty of blood on his hands to merit what Mark had done, but he still wished he hadn't had to be the one to carry out the sentence.

He left Conway's room, relieved to discover no curious tenants had gathered in the corridor. If anyone had heard his brawl with the mercenary, they'd either decided not to get involved or called the front desk to receive the furniture-moving excuse he'd left with Jan. Even so, Mark didn't want to use the elevator and pass through the hotel lobby near Jan's desk. She'd probably begun to wonder about the truth of his story by now and there wasn't anything to be gained by letting her know when he left.

The Penetrator located a flight of stairs. He prepared to descend them when he heard someone galloping up the steps. The cops? No, it sounded like only one pair of feet, probably shod in tennis shoes. He leaned over the rail and gazed down to see an old acquaintance on his way up the stairs.

Dennis Richards.

13

Questions and Answers

So the boy wonder of the hijacking world had crawled out from under his rock at last. Obviously, Dennis had come to see Roger Conway. The Penetrator swiftly and silently mounted the stairwell to the next floor and watched the kid jog up to the second story landing and make a beeline to the corridor for Conway's room.

Mark quickly crept down to the same level and considered his next move. Should he grab Dennis and try to wring some information out of him? No, he decided. When the kid found Conway dead, how would he react? He sure as hell wouldn't hang around the Callicutt Hotel for long, Mark thought as he quietly descended the stairs to the first floor.

The Penetrator slipped out a side entrance of the building and stepped into the hotel parking lot. Then he climbed into his rented Mazda and waited for Dennis. Less than five minutes passed, then the kid bolted from the hotel and dashed into the parking lot. His face pale and eyes wide with fear, Dennis glanced about as though expecting someone to pounce on him. Then he ran to a badly dented Volkswagon beetle.

"Okay, punk," Mark whispered, starting the engine of his car. "Let's see where you lead me."

The VW soon roared out of the lot and the Penetrator's Mazda followed. He carefully tailed Dennis' car, avoiding getting too close. The kid was inexperienced, but he'd just received a giant economy-size scare so he'd be suspicious of any vehicle that appeared too frequently in his rear view mirror.

He followed Dennis across the Mississippi on the Greater New Orleans bridge and then onto Patterson Street in Algirs. The kid headed for a little used pier by the river. Mark noticed the VW had slowed down before it rolled toward an old waterfront warehouse. The Penetrator drove past the building before pulling to the shoulder of the road. He got out and raised the hood to give the impression that his Mazda was a disabled vehicle, thus reducing the likelihood of attracting suspicion from any passing police car. Removing an aluminum suitcase from the trunk, he started back to the warehouse on foot.

Charles Horn, a short sour-faced gangster who smoked big, fat cigars, listened to Dennis Richards tell how he'd gone to Conway's hotel and found the mercenary recruiter dead with a metal "pen" stuck in his nose.

"Bet one of those Vietnam veterans that got hooked on dope did it," Horn remarked, his voice distorted by the cigar in his mouth. "Bet that's what happened."

Henri St. Clair, one of Jacoby's mercenaries wasn't willing to dismiss the matter in such a casual manner. He, Horn and the two muscle boys, Lou and Harry, had gathered together in the warehouse, following Linsey's orders to keep a low profile. Apparently things had gone badly on the last hijacking attempt and the cops might begin a serious investigation into the New Orleans chapter of the operation.

St. Clair, who actually out-ranked the late Captain Conway, although he'd allowed the recruiter to take the limelight—and the risks that went with it—had suggested they "hit the mattresses" for a while. So the four men had been holed up in the warehouse for a day and a half, playing poker, leafing through girlie magazines and getting on each other's nerves. St. Clair hated working with the American hoodlums. He considered Linsey to be an imbecile—and he was probably the smartest one of the lot! As for the trio which he'd been forced to share quarters with . . . *Merde alors*!

"Have you forgotten about the "mystery man" who has been causing so much trouble for us?" St. Clair inquired, lighting a cigarette. "The one who seems to be more than any of you are capable of dealing with?"

"I ain't forgot," Lou Moore growled. His right arm was still in a sling, the triceps heavily bandaged. "And you just watch your mouth, Frenchie. You don't know how tough that mutter is until you've come up against 'im like Harry and me done."

"Wait a fucking minute!" Horn suddenly snarled. He rose from a folding chair behind a card table and stomped across the room to confront Dennis. "Why'd you come here, you stupid bastard?"

The back of his hand swatted Dennis across

the mouth, knocking the boy backward into a pile of crates. "What would'da happened if that sonofabitch followed you here?"

"Probably something like this," Mark Hardin declared. He'd simply pushed open the door of the warehouse and entered, his Sidewinder held ready, with a foot-long sound-suppressor attached to the barrel.

"Shit!" Harry McKinnon cried, yanking a compact Astra .380 automatic from his hip pocket.

The silenced Sidewinder spat hoarsely and a three-round burst caught the thug in his barrel chest. The impact of the slugs hurled Harry into the crates, almost colliding with Dennis Richards. The kid would have been better off if he had. Harry's Astra was pointing at Dennis' face when a muscle spasm caused his finger to pull the trigger.

A .380 projectile drilled through the kid's left eyesocket. Harry and Dennis fell into each other and engaged in a quivering embrace of death as they sunk to the floor.

"Anybody else tired of living?" the Penetrator inquired.

The three men who remained raised their hands in surrender.

"All right," Mark nodded in satisfaction. "Everybody move to the center of the room where we can talk."

They obeyed. When he could cover the trio more easily, Mark asked them about the hijackings and which Caribbean island was targeted for the invasion.

"I ain't sayin' shit," Horn declared, his cigar wobbling in his mouth. "I wanna call my lawyer. You can't . . ."

The Sidewinder coughed harshly and Charles Horn bit through his cigar and then screamed, his plump stogie tumbling from his open lips like a well-chewed turd.

Mark had fired a burst into both of Horn's kneecaps. The crook crumpled to the floor, moaning feebly as he clutched his shattered legs.

"The Red Brigade and the IRA are famous for 'knee-capping' victims," the Penetrator commented, noticing the horrified expressions of the faces of St. Clair and Lou. "I consider you bastards to be the twin brothers to terrorists, so maybe terrorist tactics is all you'll understand."

"You can't . . ." Lou began, then realized those were Horn's exact words before Mark shot him. "We got rights . . ."

"You *had* rights," the Penetrator said sternly. "As an American citizen, you were both born with more rights and privileges than one can find anywhere in the world. But when you and your kind are willing to trample on the rights of others, you cancel out yours as far as I'm concerned . . ." He gave them a cold smile. "And I'm what you have to worry about right now. I'm not a social worker or a member of the Police Benevolent League, so you can either answer my questions or figure out how you can make down payments on a wheelchair."

"I can't tell you which island will be invaded," Henri St. Clair sighed. "But I know where the yachts have been taken and the mercenary army is being trained for the operation. It's Honduras."

Kimberly McCulley patted his IBM computer and sighed. The machine was too large to take with him to Honduras and he hated to be away from his computers for more than a day. Still, after they conquered Guadalupe, he could arrange to have the equipment shipped to his new kingdom.

"I've become rather fond of this place," he mused. "Never have come to care much for Costa Rica, but then I seldom leave these walls and I have all that I need right here."

Joe Linsey glared at McCulley when he heard the fat man's remark. He'd always considered McCulley to be a nutcase, but a brilliant one like Einstein or Hitler. The type of man who can dream the wildest schemes and make them reality. If McCulley suddenly decided to cancel the whole operation because he'd rather sit in his air-conditioned office and play with his overpriced adding machines, Linsey swore he'd shoot the lunatic right then and there.

"Well," McCulley smiled. "I don't have everything I *want*." He turned to face Linsey. "A man's wants become needs after he's grown accustomed to the better things in life, Joseph. I wonder what sort of addictions we'll acquire after we've become monarchs of a financial empire and the rulers of our own nation?"

Christ, Linsey hated it when McCulley began to slip away into his private dream world. "I've been trying to tell you about the last mission, Kim . . ."

"And I've been listening," McCulley assured him with a sigh of exasperation. "A man armed with a submachine gun was waiting for you on the yacht, he killed some of your men and blew up your boat, but you managed to get away. It's all quite unfortunate, but we still have enough vessels in our fleet to carry out the invasion, thus I don't see any real problem."

"But that son of a bitch is the Penetrator," Linsey insisted. "I'm sure of it . . . and I know *who he is.*"

"Really?" McCulley rolled his eyes in exasperation.

"Guy's name is Mark Hardin," Linsey declared with glee. "I knew about him back in Vietnam when he fouled up a black market operation we had going over there. Fucker was an Army snoop who blabbed about what we were doing to the press. Most of the Army guys involved got rugged after that, but they didn't know about me, so I never got touched." He smiled wickedly. "But I was the one who found out Hardin squealed on us. Since you never know what sort of useful information might be discussed in an AP wire service office, I'd planted an eavesdropping device behind one of the panels of a wall in the place. Nifty little transmitter with two nine-volt batteries for . . ."

"Joseph," McCulley interrupted. "None of this is important. Someone, the Penetrator or whomever, has become aware of some of our activities and decided to meddle in them. That means we'll stop hijacking boats—after all, I already said we don't need any more. Frankly, we can't afford to delay at this point. Paying the salaries of your employees as well as Colonel Jacoby's mercenary army—to say nothing of having to feed and arm those soldiers of fortune—has become a considerable strain on my financial reserves. That's why we must be on our way to Honduras to step up the date for D-Day."

"Step it up?" Linsey raised his eyebrows. "When do you figure we should do it then?"

"Oh," McCulley offered with a shrug. "I see no reason why we can't do it tomorrow."

14

Too Late?

The machete slashed at a tangle of vines and the Penetrator pushed his way through the wall of vegetation. Mark used the big jungle knife sparingly, trying to avoid any unnecessary noise as he approached the mercenary training camp in the tropical rain forest near Lake Credasco.

After questioning the hoods in New Orleans, Mark had bound and gagged the survivors and immediately headed for the airport where his Mooney 201 waited. Grateful that he had all the weapons and explosives he'd need already in the trunk of the rented Mazda, the Penetrator made an anonymous phone call to the police and informed them about the location of a warehouse full of criminals—one of whom would require immediate medical assistance while two others would only require the services of a mortician.

Then the Penetrator flew his Mooney from the runway and headed for Honduras. He hadn't planned to return to Central America for a while due to a recent mission that had taken him to Guatamala and Nicaragua and briefly into Honduras. He'd been forced to stir up quite an incident in Honduras and Guatemala, especially in the latter country, where his cover as a Special Forces captain working for the CIA had been blown. He reflected with relief that the authorities hadn't been waiting to pounce on him when the Guatemalan Coast Guard had rescued him at sea, so Mark doubted that the Honduras government would still be hoping to nail him for an unauthorized flight he'd made across their country into Nicaragua and back again.

His prediction proved correct. He'd landed in San Pedro Sula without attracting any special attention and, thanks to his excellent Spanish, had little trouble renting a jeep. Then it was simply a matter of finding Lake Credasco and Colonel Jacoby's mercenary camp. And taking it on single-handed.

However, the Penetrator carried plenty of lethal firepower when he thrashed his way through the rain forest. In addition to the Sidewinder and MatchMaster pistol, he'd brought an M-79 grenade launcher and a hip pouch full of HE shells, not to mention an assortment of hand grenades—M-34s, WPs and conclusion cannisters.

The one-man army finally hacked and slithered his way through the jungle and located his objective . . . only to discover the merc camp had been deserted.

Mark cautiously crept along the edge of the mock town where Jacoby's troops had practiced for battle against the "buildings" of flimsy poles and fishnets. He moved on to the main base and inspected each wooden billet with care.

Not a single communications clerk or radio operator remained. Mark even checked a small medic's tent in hope there might be a sick or injured mercenary left behind who could tell him where the others had gone. He found no one.

Finally, he headed for the yacht basin at Lake Credasco. A huge white sign with RENT A BEACH HOUSE AND A YACHT IN PARADISE printed in Spanish and English, seemed to mock him. Clever bastards, Mark thought. They'd hidden the stolen boats Edgar Allan Poe-style, right in the open, disguised as a tourist promotional gimmick. Christ, the Honduran government probably *helped* them set the operation up.

No matter now. The yacht basin itself was empty. The mercs hadn't even left a rowboat behind. Mark bitterly realized he'd arrived too late. The invasion force had already set sail and he still had no idea about their destination.

The Penetrator had never failed to accomplish a mission. Regardless of the odds or how formidable his opponents had been in the past, Mark had always emerged the victor and his enemies' treacherous, often bizarre schemes had fallen into shambles.

He'd conducted missions within enemy countries, such as Persis and North Korea. Mark had come up against conspiracies to overthrow the United States or even conquer the world. Now, a single Caribbean island was about to fall victim to a ruthless invasion—and if St. Clair's information had been accurate, the entire operation had been planned, organized and financed by a single man, whose identity still remained a mystery. And the Penetrator was powerless to stop it.

"You sons of bitches haven't won yet," he growled. He'd done too much, come too close to

success, to accept defeat. Clell Brockman and
Cindy Brown and probably a dozen other innocent victims of the hijackers would not go
unavenged.

His determination restored, Mark marched
back to the mercenary base. If he could find one
clue—a mark on a map, reconnaissance photo-
graphs or a single report on the invasion target
area—then there'd still be a chance to rob the
pirates of their conquest and pay them back,
blood for blood.

The Penetrator had little trouble recognizing
which billet had formerly been used by Colonel
Jacoby for his headquarters. Equipped with office furniture, wall charts with troop training
activity schedules and a detailed map of the
Caribbean, its function was obvious.

He checked the wall map first, but failed to
find a single penstroke or pinhole to suggest an
invasion site. A jagged piece of clear plastic nailed
to the wall above the map explained why. A
transparent sheet had hung over the map to
allow the mercs to draw diagrams of the invasion route and target with a grease pencil.
Obviously, they'd ripped off the plastic and destroyed it for security purposes.

The Penetrator opened a filing cabinet and
found a ship's chandlery catalog, a number of
field manuals and tech manuals in English,
French, Spanish and German, and some more
maps. He dumped the material on the desk and
hastily searched through the catalog and maps.
Nothing had been marked, underlined or circled.

Then he searched the desks. Every drawer
proved to be empty except one, which contained
a half-full pint bottle of Jamaican rum. There

had to be something that could serve as a clue. He twisted off the aluminum cap and took a long pull on the Appleton's in search of inspiration.

Mark left the head shed. Maybe a drunken merc had scrawled some graffiti on an outhouse wall that declared "We'll kick ass in the Virgin Islands" or "Dominica or Bust." He was so preoccupied with his thoughts, Mark almost ran into a large metal trash burner.

He stopped abruptly when he felt heat radiate from the converted 55 gallon oil drum. Peering inside, Mark discovered the barrel contained fresh ashes with a few charred pieces of paper jutting from the gray and black mounds.

"Never thought I'd end up rummaging through trash cans," he muttered, tipping over the drum.

The Penetrator searched through the burned remains of an assortment of maps, documents and notes. He stomped on some still-glowing ashes, realizing the papers had only recently been set on fire. That meant the invasion force had probably left Lake Credasco minutes before he'd arrived.

At last, he discovered a charred scrap of paper that listed several landing zones and beaches. Quickly, the Penetrator rushed back inside the HQ building and opened the navigator's rudder log he'd left on Jacoby's desk.

"Okay," he said to himself, poring over the maps and tables in the Caribbean section. "Now if this information jells . . ."

"Guadalupe!" he shouted. "The bastards plan to hit Point-a-Pitre and storm over the island before the people of Guadalupe get a chance to catch their breath."

Could the nameless madman's private assault force possibly carry out his wild scheme? A tiny speck of an island located between Antigua and Dominica, Guadalupe would indeed be vulnerable to an unexpected invasion. What sort of chance would she have against an army of professional soldiers? Even if the Penetrator could alert the French protectorate in time, the odds would remain overwhelmingly in favor of the pirates.

It almost sounded like a baseball game— the Independent Pirates take on the Caribbean Islanders. If a player is struck out it's for keeps. A home run will consist of taking about a dozen lives and no umpire will be around to call a foul. The winner of the game gets to claim Guadalupe in the end. The loser won't be in any condition to file a complaint to the International Warfare Commission.

One thing was certain, the Penetrator couldn't afford to waste another minute in Honduras.

15

"Such A Thing Cannot Be!"

Marcel LeTrec frowned. The expression seemed to make all his features sag in a typically Gallic manner. The bags under his eyes, the long, over-sized nose and the double chin beneath his pouting, full lower lip all drooped dramatically when the corners of his mouth turned down. Guadalupe's deputy minister of security balefully gazed up at the tall dark man who claimed to belong to some sort of federal police force in *les Etats Unis*.

"*Monsieur*," he began with a weary sigh. "You claim to have just flown here from Honduras and you wish to warn us of this plot to invade our island. *Oui*?"

"That's right," Mark Hardin replied, frustraton boiling inside him.

The Penetrator's plane had left San Pedro Sula like a guided missile. He'd pushed the Mooney 201 as though flying a fighter jet in order to reach Guadalupe before the mercenaries hit the island.

He'd actually seen the assault force from the air. Mark had to give the mastermind who'd conjured up the scheme credit. The fleet of blue water boats appeared to be as harmless as they were graceful, cutting across the Caribbean Sea

toward the Lesser Antilles in a rather casual
V-shaped formation. Smaller power boats rode
along with the yachts, two remaining ahead of
the main force while the others stayed with the
formation. The Penetrator counted a dozen yachts
and twice that many power boats, as well as a
small fishing trawler that remained at the rear
of the fleet, along with a rust-bucket coastal
steamer.

If only he'd been flying a fighter equipped
with bombs and machine guns, he could have
wiped out most of the fleet right there and then.
Unfortunately, Mark's Mooney wasn't designed
for combat, so he merely flew over the vessels
and kept his altitude high enough to avoid
suspicion. It would have been natural enough
for the pilot of a small private plane to draw
closer for a good look at such a collection of
beautiful boats, but if the pirates had mounted
machine guns or rocket launchers in plain view,
they might have blasted him out of the sky to
prevent him from reporting this information via
radio.

After his brief and incomplete recon, the
Penetrator continued to Guadalupe. His plane
touched down on a runway near Basse-Terre,
the capital of the island, and Mark wasted no
time contacting the authorities. The Penetrator
soon found himself in the deputy minister of
security's office—facing yet another obstacle.

"But, *Monsieur* Banner," LaTrec continued.
"Why would Honduras wish to invade Guada-
lupe? This makes no more sense than to suggest
Mexico would wish to invade Honolulu."

"Honduras isn't attacking your island," Mark

tried to explain the situation for the third time, wishing his French was as fluent as his Spanish. "An army of mercenaries are on their way here in a fleet of yachts . . ."

"Yachts?" LeTrec queried with a raised eyebrow and a cynical smile. "And armed with shuffleboard *batons, oui?*"

The Penetrator struggled to control his temper while the door to LaTrec's office opened and a tall, lean man dressed in a blue khaki version of a French police uniform, entered. "*Deputé LaTrec . . .*" the man began before he noticed Mark. "Oh . . . *Pardon. J'e retour plus tard, Monsieur.*"

"*Non, Capitaine* Arnaud," LeTrac replied, urging the man to stay. "Perhaps you should stay and listen to this. Our visitor from *les Etats Unis* claims we are about to be invaded by *mercenaires* on yachts who will throw deck furniture at us when they arrive. *C'est magnifique!*"

"Damn it!" the Penetrator snapped. "I've been trying to get this through your thick bureaucratic head for the last twenty minutes!" Mark's anger startled the Guadalupians. "A private army, under command of a British mercenary named Colonel Jacoby, is going to arrive at the beaches of Point-a-Pitre and attack this island like a pack of wolves in a herd of sheep—and apparently the shepherds are just going to sit on their asses and let it happen."

"And you are a *crier au loup* who has come all the way from America—*non*, just from Honduras, correct?" LaTrec snorted in reply.

"I told you who I am," Mark insisted. "I showed you my Justice Department identification . . ."

"You have no authority on Guadalupe, *Monsieur*," LaTrec declared, thrusting a finger at the Penetrator. "If indeed your identification is not false."

"Why do you think I'm here?" Mark continued. "I've already explained about the yacht hijackings I investigated in my country which led me to Honduras and to the invasion plot I'm trying to warn you about. And ... you'd better wake up and listen, LaTrec," he warned, then took a glance at his watch. "Because my guess is those boats will be arriving in about two more hours, which doesn't give us long to prepare."

"*Sacrebleu*!" the deputy minister exclaimed. "I have heard enough of this *nonsens*!"

"Perhaps we should not respond too harhsly too quickly, *Deputé*," Captain Arnaud began. "I have heard of this *mercenaire*, Jacoby, when I was with the French National Police in Paris ..."

"*Oui, Capitaine*," LaTrec rolled his eyes. "And your former duty in France was far more colorful and interesting than anything we can offer you on this dull little island"

Arnaud took the sarcasm in stride. "Jacoby is real, *Deputé* LaTrec."

"*Et alors*?" the bureaucrat demanded. "There is a magazine in *les Etats Unis* printed for would-be *Legionnaries*. Banner could have learned of this British adventurer by simply reading an article about him."

"How do you explain the fleet of boats that are approaching Guadalupe at this very minute?" the Penetrator asked, incredulously. "Do you think I went to this much trouble just to play an elaborate hoax?"

"You *Americains* are famous for your strange sense of humor and an over-active imagination," LaTrec dismissed it. "No private army would invade Guadalupe in yachts. It is absurd! They would not dare to incur the wrath of our international protector—*La Belle France*!"

He said the last word in such an explosive nasal manner that the Penetrator expected to see a disgusting display spew from LaTec's nostrils. Mark realized the situation was pointless. Would the empty-headed bureaucrat start humming the Marseilles next? He shrugged off his anger. "Thanks for your time, LaTrec," he muttered, heading for the door.

"*Monsieur!*" the deputy minister snapped, his voice halting Mark. "If you wish to remain in Guadalupe, I suggest you refrain from uttering such nonsense. We can deport you back to the United States. *Comprendez-vous*?"

"*Oui, merde-tete,*" the Penetrator replied. He wasn't certain if he'd said the insult in proper French, but LaTrec appeared to be adequately offended, so he knew he'd come close enough.

Mark Hardin strode angrily from the government building, thoroughly disgusted with Gallic stubbornness and tunnel vision. Yet, in all honesty, he couldn't fault LaTrec for finding a tale of an invasion force sailing to Point-a-Pitre in a fleet of pretty white yachts hard to believe. The incredible nature of the assault was, in fact, exactly why it would succeed.

LaTrec seemed to think he could wave the French flag and protect Guadalupe via its status as a protectorate of the European nation. Even

if France did respond by galloping into the
Caribbean as England had in the Falkland Islands—and Mark personally doubted this would
occur—it would be too late for the people of
Guadalupe.

"*Attendez vous, s'il vous plait,*" a voice called
softly. Mark turned to see Captain Arnaud emerge
from the building. "Please, I wish to speak with
you, *Monsieur.*"

"I think your boss has said it all, Captain,"
the Penetrator sighed, but he waited for Arnaud
to catch up with him.

"We were not properly introduced," the captain stated. Although an inch and a half taller
than Mark, he was considerably less muscular.
He extended a long-fingered hand and said, "I
am Gaston Arnaud."

"James Banner," Mark replied, noting the
strength of Arnaud's grip when they shook hands.
"Thanks for trying to help back there."

"I'm afraid LaTrec has been an official in a
small and seldom disturbed position for too long
to see a potential threat and recognize it for
what it is. Besides, he hates Americans." Arnaud
shrugged. "I, however, know that bizarre plots
do occur. This is not your first experience with a
conspiracy, *oui*?"

"I've been in law enforcement for some time,"
Mark allowed, but he didn't like the sly smile on
Gaston's lean face.

"When I was still a policeman in France,"
Arnaud began. "I nearly encountered *le Penetrator*,
a famous American crime fighter, in Marseilles,
where he had killed an international assassin in
a gunfight. Later, in Paris, I barely missed him

again. Incredibly enough, he had killed four dwarfs in a sword duel at the Eiffel Tower."

"Were the other three still with Snow White?" Mark scoffed, trying to dispel the cold finger of certainty that crawled his spine.

"It is a pleasure to finally meet you, *Monsieur Penetrator*," Gaston declared.

"Jesus!" Mark muttered. "Where'd you get a notion like that? I'm with the Justice Department, OCN . . ."

"That does not explain your presence here in Guadalupe," Gaston insisted. "Arriving in a private aircraft."

"I came to this island to try to warn you about the pirates."

"And I believe your story, *Monsieur Penetrator*."

"Nuts!" Mark groaned. "Will you stop calling me that? My Name's Jim, but if you want to think I'm the Penetrator, or Batman, I don't care, so long as you're willing to help do something about this invasion."

"Very well, Jim," Gaston relented. "I have friends at Point-a-Pitre among the fishermen as well as the local police. I'm certain I can convince them of the danger and we can put together a defense force to combat the mercenaries."

The Penetrator grimaced. Fishermen and a handful of island cops against a hundred and fifty trained soldiers of fortune—some contest.

Arnaud read Mark's expression correctly. "Is there any other choice of action, *mon ami*?" he asked, displaying the classical palms-up, flamboyant shrug that is Gallic body language crudely translated as "fuck it."

"Yeah," Mark replied, agreeing with Gaston's gesture as well as his words. "Whatever we do, we'd better do it *fast*."

"*Oui*," the captain confirmed.

16

Pirate Armada

Kimberly McCulley gazed down at his fleet from the bridge of the "mother-ship," an old tramp steamer—the largest and best armed, if slowest, vessel in his armada. He smiled. No one had ever commanded a navy similar to his. The blue water boats had been magnificent toys for the wealthy until he'd converted them into battle ships.

True alchemy, he thought with pride, consists of brilliant ideas and planning, not metallurgical tricks. He had taken the frivolous and made it useful. He'd transmuted harmless objects and made them deadly. He'd transformed a dream into reality.

These were not matters to share with the men under his command, he realized, most of whom consisted of petty gangsters and free-lance soldiers familiar only with achieving goals through the use of brute force. Such intellectual cripples would always be subservient to a man of vision for they had no concept of real power nor appreciation for the genius required to get it. McCulley flicked on the switch to a PA system and spoke into a microphone.

"We have reached the Lesser Antilles," his voice bellowed from the loudspeakers to every vessel in his armada. "We will be approaching the beaches of Guadalupe in approximately one hour."

A collective cheer roared from the surrounding boats. McCulley felt a tingle of excitement rush up his backbone. If those brutish dolts who'd mocked him as a child could see him now! The funny fat little boy with a girl's name had become a modern Hannibal. His troops saluted him like gladiators before Nero. They honored his position and brilliance. McCulley knew how Hitler and Stalin must have felt, when they'd stood before adoring masses that thrust stiff arms into the air or raised clenched fists in homage to their leader.

"By nightfall," McCulley continued, managing to keep his voice authoratative and void of emotion, "We shall have conquered an island and claimed more than mere territory in the process. Gentlemen, we are about to become a nation unto ourselves. We will make our own laws and be impervious to those of other countries. We are twentieth century Vikings and we shall live as kings never dreamed possible."

Another cheer echoed from the armada. Joe Linsey and Colonel Treaver Jacoby had made a personal truce since their last meeting in Honduras. They stood behind McCulley on the bridge, two very different men who shared a common position as his seconds in command.

"If he tells me to wear one of those hats with the horns stickin' outta it," Linsey whispered to the colonel, "he can go fuck himself.

Jacoby smiled. "This is a pep rally for the

troops," he explained. "Our Mr. McCulley understands the type of men who belong to my mercenary army. All this romantic rot about Vikings and kings is just the sort of adventurer's propaganda that fuels the spirits of such chaps."

"Figure we can pull this off?" Linsey inquired.

Jacoby turned to him. "Take Guadalupe? Yes, indeed. However, we'll have to watch that Mr. McCulley doesn't get any silly notions about seizing other islands to extend his activities."

"No problem," Linsey assured him. "Kim plans to use Guadalupe as a base for financial operations. You've heard him. Taking over land doesn't appeal to him."

"Not yet," Jacoby agreed. "But he's never conquered any before. The thrill of conquest can become addictive, Mr. Linsey. I know. Why do you think I'm in this business?"

When the cheers died down, McCulley incited them one last time by concluding with, "Now, on to victory."

Alchemy, he thought, switching off the PA system. Soon, he would transform an unproductive and obscure island into a seat of international power—with himself on the throne.

Armand Jordan, a short bull-like fisherman, strode across the sand and joined Mark Hardin and Gaston Arnaud who were busy pumping oxygen from a welder's tank into a 55 gallon oil drum. Jorgan gaped at them, totally confused by their actions.

"Are the boats ready, Armand?" Gaston asked, inserting a tube-shaped object into the spout of the drum.

"Oui," Jordan replied. "What are you doing here?"

"We're preparing a few surprises for the pirates," the Penetrator answered. He gestured at five barrels identical to the one he and Gaston had been working with. "These drums are one-eighth full of gasoline, which is then enriched by pumping in oxygen. Makes one hell of a bang, about the same as two cases of dynamite."

"Sacrebleau!" the fisherman stared at the drums as though he feared they might explode right in front of him.

"Don't worry, *mon ami,"* Gaston assured him. "These will not go off until a certain frequency is transmitted to the radio detonators inserted in each barrel. However, I do not advise you to smoke around them. *Comprendez vous?"*

"Oui," Jordan nodded woodenly. "Another of your inventions, *Monsieur?"* he directed at Mark.

"Let's say I've picked up a trick or two, Armand," the Penetrator returned, smiling.

En effet, this "James Banner" knew many such "tricks." Jordan and the other fishermen had been instructed in the manufacture of impoverished napalm grenades by this mysterious *Americain.* He'd taught them how to use motor oil, gelatin powder and laundry detergent to thicken gasoline for that purpose. They would be hearing about the raids on kitchens from their wives for an eternity, *zut alors!* Banner had inspected the assortment of shotguns, rifles and sharkguns the fishermen owned, advising them about each weapon's potential in combat.

Although Gaston Arnaud and Wilhelm Champmaison, the Point-a-Pitre Chief of Police, were involved in organizing and supervising the defense force against the invasion, "James Banner" was clearly in command. The *Americain* had hastily put together a strategy for the others, revealing a remarkable knowledge and ability that obviously had been acquired by personal experience.

Champmaison, a half-German blond who seemed totally out of place among the swarthy fishermen of pure French descent, supplied two dozen police officers. Mark had been surprised and pleased to discover the cops were armed with grenade launchers and tear gas or riot control grenades, as well as MAT-49 submachine guns, although some officers—Champmaison included—preferred pump shotguns.

The chief of police raised an eyebrow when he saw the Penetrator's Sidewinder and M-79 grenade launcher, but didn't ask any questions. Champmaison seemed equally unconcerned about any local "gun control" violations by the fishermen as well. Mark's kind of cop.

"How much time do we have left to prepare, *Monsieur*?" Champmaison inquired.

"I don't know," the Penetrator admitted. "Damn little. We're getting close to the wire and the opposition is going to come sailing toward us any minute now."

"All the more reason for us to hurry and get everything aboard the boats, Jim," Gaston declared. "We can't . . ."

Suddenly a uniformed figure on a motorcycle cut across the beach toward them. Champmaison frowned when he noticed it was a dispatch rider from his department.

"*Qu'est-ce que c'est*, DeVolt?" he demanded.

"Message de Capitaine Arnaud," the dispatch rider explained, kicking on the motorcycle brake.

"Merci," Gaston said, taking the note from DeVolt. He hastily read the message and turned to Mark. "It is from *Deputé Minister* LeTrec."

Champmaison muttered, *"Merde,"* and the Penetrator was inclined to agree with him.

"You judge him too harshly," Gaston stated. "LeTrec may be a 'stuffed shirt,' as one might say in Jim's country, but he loves Guadalupe and wishes no harm to come to her. Apparently he guessed I had left with Jim for Point-a-Pitre when he discovered I was not in my office at Basse-Terre. Although he still does not believe this invasion is a genuine threat, he urges us to take every possible precaution because a large number of boats has been spotted on radar, approaching Guadalupe from the northwest. He adds that it is possible the *Americain* Banner's claims may be correct."

"Well," the Penetrator sighed. "That tells us something about how much time we have left. Not enough to waste any of it on this beach."

"Oui," Champmaison agreed. He promptly ordered his men into the boats that waited at the beach.

"Jim," Gaston began. "Are you certain it is best to fight these *mercenaires* at sea? Most of our force is comprised of fishermen, not soldiers."

"That's exactly why their chances will be better at sea," Mark explained.

"Many of them will be killed before this is over," Gaston complained. "I know this is rather late, but couldn't we set up an ambush here at the beach?"

"We'd never stop them that way, Gaston," the

Penetrator answered. "The mercenaries have been trained to assault the island *after* they get off the ships. If we can catch them unprepared before they reach dry land, we might have enough of an advantage to tip the odds in our favor."

"The odds are not good, are they?" Gaston asked grimly.

Mark shrugged. "We'll find out soon enough."

17

Battle For Paradise

The pirate armada approached Guadalupe. Colonel Jacoby ordered the mercenaries to prepare to hit the beaches. Kimberly McCulley stood at the bow of the tramp steamer to get his first good look at the island that would soon belong to him.

"What are all those boats doing out there?" he demanded, turning sharply to face Joe Linsey.

"Hell, Kim," Linsey grunted. "those are just a bunch of fishing boats."

To humor McCulley, he raised a pair of binoculars and inspected the Gudalupian vessels. He couldn't see much of the crews on board, but he noticed a sleek 36 foot Chriscraft and some sort of police or coast guard patrol boat mixed in with the fishing fleet. Hardly anything to get excited about. The fuzz were probably there to chew somebody out for littering on the high seas. Linsey had noticed several discarded oil drums bobbing around in the water.

He failed to consider the fact that the barrels formed a line between the invasion fleet and the fishing vessels—or that the latter remained not less than two hundred yards away from the drums—might be important.

On board the Chriscraft, the Penetrator, Gaston Arnaud and a Point-a-Pitre patrolman named Jules Gelee, who piloted the boat, observed the advancing armada. Mark lowered his Bushnell binoculars and announced that the pirates would soon be in position.

Gaston watched the Penetrator pick up a walkie-talkie. "We are going to give them a chance to surrender first, *oui*?"

"Just as soon as we give them a reason to," Mark replied, extending the two-way radio's antenna. "Champmaison? Armond? Is everyone in position?"

The cop and the fisherman both replied in the affirmative. Mark gazed over his fleet—consisting of fourteen fishing boats of various shapes and sizes, the Chriscraft and the patrol boat—as he listened to the voices of Champmaison and Jordan from the walkie-talkie. The enemy vessels outnumbered them more than two against one.

"Okay," he spoke into the hand radio. "Fireworks are about to begin."

The Penetrator put down the communications device and picked up another type of radio, a remote-control signal box. With his thumb poised above the switch, he raised the Bushnells and watched the armada close in.

Two motor boat scouts passed between the fifty-five gallon drums that floated in the path of the assault force. Mark waited until the first two yachts had reached the barrels before he flicked the switch. The remote control sent a high frequency signal to the radio detonators installed in the improvised mines. Three drums exploded simultaneously.

One yacht was ripped to pieces by the blast

which occurred literally under her keel. The boat seemed to shatter like a giant ivory carving that had been dropped off the top of the Empire State Building to the pavement below. Another mine only served to send a violent geyser into the air in front of the pirates' craft. However, the third bomb erupted between a yacht and an advancing motorboat, blowing a huge hole in the hull of the former and smashing the latter into kindling, hurtling three dismembered mercenary corpses across the Caribbean.

"Three out of three's not bad," Mark opined.

On board the tramp steamer, McCulley and his crew stared in amazement and horror at the unexpected destruction of three vessels in their fleet. Kimberly McCulley grabbed the PA system microphone.

"Attack those boats!" he ordered. "Kill every son of a bitch on board!"

"Are you insane?" Colonel Jacoby snapped, rushing into the radio room. "We aren't prepared to do battle with an enemy fleet at sea!"

"What are you talking about?" McCulley demanded, thrusting his hands into the pockets of his white Haggard slacks. "Those are just a bunch of fishing boats and we far outnumber them. You mean your men can't take them?"

"Of course we can," Jacoby replied. "But we have no way of knowing how well armed they might be. The battle could cost too many lives for us to retain enough personnel to successfully complete the invasion."

"And there for a minute, I thought you were concerned about your men," Linsey muttered.

"The mission comes before anything else," Jacoby stated, like the true professional soldier he was. "And this is one mission that has to be canceled immediately!"

McCulley then did something neither the colonel nor Joe Linsey had expected him capable of. He calmly drew a diminutive NAM mini-revolver from his pocket. Less than four inches in overall length, the tiny gun looked like a stainless steel finger jutting from McCulley's pudgy fist. He pointed the NAM directly at Colonel Jacoby's face.

"How would you handle a mutiny, Colonel?" McCulley asked quietly.

Then he shot Jacoby in the face. The first .22 long rifle bullet struck the merc commander in the left cheek, cracking bone before ripping up his tongue. Moving faster than anyone would have imagined possible for an obese intellectual, McCulley cocked and fired the NAM into the hollow of Jacoby's throat when his head snapped back from the impact of the first round. McCulley shot him a third time between the eyes.

The colonel was already dead when his body fell against the door frame of the radio room and began to slide to the deck. McCulley casually put another .22 through Jacoby's left temple and then fired the last round into the back of his head. Joe Linsey and several other witnesses watched, stunned by McCulley's actions. The fat man knelt beside his victim and removed Jacoby's sidearm, an old .38 caliber Long Colt.

"I trust I've made my point to all of you," he remarked calmly, discarding the empty NAM in favor of the colonel's revolver. "We're not turning back. I've invested too much into this operation and planned too long to give it up now."

"Holy shit," Linsey whispered, wondering what sort of mess he'd gotten himself into. "And just when Jacoby and me were starting to get along, too."

Perhaps if the bulk of the assault force had been aware of Col. Jacoby's impromptu execution, they would have retreated. However, with the majority of the men scattered among the smaller crafts, and ignorant of this knowledge, they charged across the water toward the Penetrator's fleet.

The two scout motor boats kept the lead. Both contained three mercenaries, one to pilot the vessel and two men to handle an H&K 21A1 machine gun mounted on an L-1102 tripod. The weapons began to spray the fishing boats with 5.56mm hail while the rest of the pirate fleet continued to advance.

The mercs on board the two scout boats weren't prepared for two problems that waited for them among the defenders' forces. Police Chief Champmaison, a hard-nosed anti-communist who worried about pro-Castro terrorist activity in the Caribbean the way a man with a beautiful wife frets about her fidelity, had encouraged his men to take SWAT training in every subjet from karate to scaling the sides of buildings. Thus, the Point-a-Pitre cops had several trained snipers in their ranks. A marksman with an Interarms Mark X rifle and a Bushnell 3×9 scope, popped a .300 Winchester Magnum round into the forehead of the mercenary machine gunner.

Of course, the other big problem for the scout boats—and the entire pirate armada—was the

Penetrator. Mark Hardin selected his M-79 to deal with the merc power boats. He followed the circular movement of one of the scout vessels, tracked it with the grenade launcher and fired.

An HE projectile sailed into the power boat like a perfectly thrown basketball landing in the hoop. The grenade set off the gas tanks and the craft exploded in a collage of violent death. Seconds later, two more sniper bullets exterminated the remaining occupants of the first scout boat.

The Penetrator adjusted the frequency of the remote control box and flicked the switch again. Anchored by weighted ropes, the three remaining fifty-five gallon drums Mark had converted into mines still lurked beneath the surface. The pirate armada was right on top of them when the bombs detonated.

Another yacht burst into a supernova of wreckage—amply decorated with human debris. Two motor boats suddenly executed somersaults and flipped over in the water, spilling their mercenary crews in the process.

"Champmaison, Jordan," Mark spoke into his walkie-talkie. "It is time to advance and engage the enemy."

Both fleets drew closer and the battle continued, but now, the Penetrator realized, the element of surprise had been exhausted. His side had been able to avoid casualties thus far, a situation that would surely change in a matter of seconds.

Mark's prediction became grim reality when a merc team on one of the yachts fired a LAW rocket launcher at the Penetrator's armada. The anti-tank projectile sizzled through the air and pierced the hull at the bow of a fishing vessel.

The boat erupted like Mt. St. Helens at sea. Not a single man on board survived.

The Penetrator's Chriscraft advanced toward the pirates and immediately attracted the murderous attention of two merc motor boats. A pair of swift wolves on the water, the enemy craft attacked from both sides of the Chriscraft, trying to get Mark's boat in a deadly crossfire.

Five-fifty-six millimeter rounds ripped into the Chriscraft, splintering wood and shattering glass. Mark and Gaston ducked in time to avoid being chopped to pieces by the lethal metal rain. Jules Gelee, however, didn't manage to follow their example in time. The Point-a-Pitre cop's body convulsed wildly behind the wheel of the Chriscraft as bullets slammed into him from two directions simultaneously.

The merc boats spun around in twin circles to try again. Then Mark and Gaston rose and hit them back. The Penetrator's Sidewinder blasted two pirates before they could adjust the tripod mount of their H&K chatterbox. He angrily noticed the mercenaries wore green fatigue uniforms with black berets, similar to U.S. Army Rangers.

Mark locked eyes with the terrified pilot of the power boat who turned to see his comrades dead and the Penetrator's subgun pointed at him. The Sid McQueen superweapon roared again and another soldier of fortune was on his way to the Big NCO Club in the Sky.

Gaston Arnaud caught the other boat under similar circumstances, except the machine gun team was furiously trying to clear their weapon, which had jammed. The Frenchman raised his MAT-49 and sprayed the mercs with 9mm destruction. Their bodies hopped and danced from the impact of the slugs. One pirate fell over the sides. The sharks would have quite a feast when this was over, Gaston thought. *Bon appetit, requins.*

The *blam* of another LAW rocket leaving the muzzle of a pirate's bazooka-style weapon drew Mark's attention in time to see the smoke-trail of the projectile a moment before it claimed another fishing boat. The vessel exploded in a horrendous display of hellfire and death.

"Gaston," the Penetrator instructed. "Take the wheel and get closer to that son of a bitch with the rocket launcher. We've got to put him out of action *now*!"

Gaston stepped over the bullet-ravaged corpse of Jules Gelee and took over as pilot while the Penetrator broke open his M-79 and loaded it with a special silver-topped cartridge grenade. The Chriscraft shot across the water, headed for the yacht with the LAW team.

Due to the back-blast of the LAW, the other pirates among the crew had to stand clear of the rocket team. One of them saw the Chriscraft approach and shouted at the men handling the rocket tube. Everyone frantically began to change positions. They were still trying when the Penetrator fired his M-79 and lopped a 40mm grenade right in their collective lap.

The HE round exploded with colossal destruction and spewed shrapnel across the yacht's decks. Flames quickly engulfed the boat and the lovely white sail became a fiery shroud attached to a burning pole. Screams from crew members who'd been unfortunate enough to survive the initial blast pierced the chatter of gunfire and exploding grenades as the two fleets continued fierce battle.

Mortar rounds belched from the foredeck of the tramp steamer. Most of the projectiles missed their targets, but another fishing boat was smashed by the volley and a fifth vessel received enough damage to put her out of the fight. Within a matter of minutes, the Penetrator's fleet and the pirate armada clashed at close quarters. The mercs couldn't use their mortars or rocket launchers under such circumstances, since few of them cared for the idea of blowing themselves to bits along with their opponents.

Despite this condition, the odds remained in favor of the pirates. They still outnumbered the Penetrator's force and they were better armed than the fishermen and Point-a-Pitre police. Two mercs with a 5.56mm Stoner machine gun chopped down half a dozen Guadalupians before one of Champmaison's sharpshooters took the gunner out with a bullet in the head.

Mercenaries hurled grenades at the fishing boats—then gasped in horrified surprise when the defenders responded in the same manner, throwing bottle bombs full of the Penetrator's home-brewed napalm or regular grenades Mark had provided for the occasion. Ripped and bloodied corpses, often missing limbs or heads, sailed into the Caribbean sky. Jagged wreckage floated on the sea and scarlet patches began to spread amid the flotsam. Flames leaped from a dozen blood-smeared decks and began to flicker ominously over the heavy slick of fuel and oil on the tossing waves.

Mark's M-79 fired a pair of incendiary rounds at two more yachts. Added to the victims of the napalm "grenades," four enemy boats were drifting aimlessly among the warring vessels, their decks and sails fully ablaze, their crews either dead or abandoned. Like four funeral ships for Viking kings, the burning craft wandered from the battle and headed for Valhalla.

A salvo of grenades sailed from one of the fishing boats and pelted the decks of a forty foot ketch. CN/CD tear gas immediately covered the yacht in a dense green fog. The fishing boat closed in while the pirates were still coughing and puking from the surprise tactic. Champmaison and a handful of other Point-a-Pitre cops leaped from their craft to the ketch, each wearing a gas mask and armed with a shotgun or MAT-49. It was a bizarre sight—six snout-faced, bug-eyed science fiction creatures assaulting a ship Errol Flynn-style.

Two power boats attacked the fishing trawler commanded by Armand Jordan. The three mercs on each craft tried identical tactics. One man piloted the boat, another fired at the larger vessel with an AKM assault rifle while a third prepared to throw a grenade when they drew within range.

Fishermen armed with .22 rifles and .30-30 Marlins shot down one of the AKM gunners and the grenade man on one of the boats. The pilot nearly collided with the side of *le Voyager*, Jordan's boat. Armand watched the power boat cut a circle in the water and grabbed up the nearest weapon at hand. He calmly aimed a speargun at the merc's exposed back. The weapon hissed when he squeezed the trigger and the mini-harpoon pierced between the pirate's shoulder blades.

"Arranger vous, couchón!" Jordan stated with satisfaction when he saw the merc's body twist violently with the spear lodged in his spine and then slump from behind the wheel.

The second pirate boat nearly reached its destination. The AKM gunner continued to supply cover fire while his partner prepared to hurl a grenade at *le Voyager*. Then a large dark cloud seemed to fly from the fishing boat and hurl toward them like an attacking swarm of bees. Too late, they realized what the thrown object was when the heavy fishing net fell upon the small boat and knocked over the rifleman and the grenade thrower.

"Oh, Christ!" a voice exclaimed. "I dropped it!"

"What . . .?" another merc replied before the grenade exploded.

Mark Hardin's Sidewinder fired a burst of .45 slugs into the side of another power boat. The pilot panicked, cut away sharply and sped nose-first into the hull of a yacht. The smaller craft split in two after smashing a huge hole in the trim sloop. The Penetrator saw two figures move at the bow of the yacht and raised his submachine gun. He held his fire when he recognized Champmaison, who was beating hell out of one of the mercs.

The cop hit his opponent with a solid left hook and pivoted with the movement of his arm to follow up with a fast *savate* side-kick that sent the pirate flying backward, over the rail and into the Caribbean. Champmaison saw Mark and gave him a thumbs up sign that his men had subdued the enemies on board the yacht.

The Penetrator replied with a thumb and forefinger "OK" symbol.

Gaston accelerated the Chriscraft toward the tramp steamer which served as the pirates' "mother ship." However, two more speed boats quickly moved in to intercept them ... permanently.

The Penetrator fired the remaining rounds from the Sidewinder's magazine and forced the crew of the first boat to duck while Gaston pulled the pin from an M-34 grenade. The Frenchman abandoned the wheel of the Chriscraft and accurately tossed the M-34 into the passing enemy vessel. The power boat began to circle around for another attack, then the grenade went off and blasted craft and crew into mangled, charred ruin.

"Not bad, eh?" Gaston remarked brightly, returning to the wheel. "Perhaps I should be a *lanceur* with one of your *Americain* baseball ..."

A sudden burst of automatic fire from the second power boat terminated Gaston's sentence. Bullets ripped at the frame of the Chriscraft and three ragged holes appeared in Gaston's chest before he fell to the bottom of the boat.

Mark nearly swung the Sidewinder toward the enemy craft, although aware it was out of ammo. The Chriscraft began to swerve out of control, so he hastily grabbed the wheel and watched the merc power boat circle around for another attack.

"You guys want me," he hissed through clenched teeth. "You're about to get me ..."

He accelerated the Chriscraft and shot forward, speeding straight at the pirate's boat. The startled mercenaries hadn't expected to play "chicken" with the Penetrator. The pilot desperately tried to steer out of Mark's path while he awkwardly attempted to fire his M-16 rifle at the Chriscraft, no small feat since both boats were moving rapidly.

A head-on collision seemed inevitable until the pirates swung to the east and Mark turned to the west. The Penetrator cut around sharply and headed right back for the disoriented mercs. Before the enemy vessel could react to his unexpected maneuver, the Penetrator hit them broadside with the Chriscraft, literally running over the pirate boat.

Wood and fiberglass crunched from the impact and the screams of the mercenaries were lost amid the crash of the brutal contact. One pirate was crushed between the two vessels, another floated on his back with a foot-long splinter stuck in the hollow of his throat. Mark spotted the third, frantically trying to swim away from the wreckage. The Penetrator drew his Match-Master .45 from a hip holster, took careful aim and fired two bullets into the fleeing figure's back.

"Jim . . .?" Gaston rasped weakly.

"I'm here," Mark replied, kneeling beside the injured man. "Just lie still and . . ."

"Die?" Gaston laughed harshly. He began to choke and turned his head to one side and spat out a mouthful of blood. "It doesn't feel good, this dying, but then the pain will end when I'm finished . . . *oui*?"

"Jesus, Gaston . . ." Mark began, but what could he tell him? You're right, buddy. You've been shot in both lungs. Don't know how you've managed to stay conscious so long. Got a wife or a sweetheart? I'm sure she'll want to know how well you died.

"*Sans important . . .*" Gaston gasped. His face twisted at the fiery agony in his chest. "Yet, I would like to know . . . one thing . . . you are *le Penetrator. Oui?*"

"You were right all along, Gaston," Mark admitted. "And I've never had the honor of fighting with a braver man than you by my side."

"Ah . . . *merci*," Gaston Arnaud raised a faltering hand and Mark took it. "*Bonne chance, mon ami . . .* good luck, my . . ."

Mark felt Gaston's grip tighten for a moment and then relax. The Penetrator folded the dead man's hands on his bullet-torn chest. "Friend," he finished the sentence Gaston had not lived to complete.

"*Monsieur* Banner? *Monsieur?*" Armand Jordan's voice spoke from the walkie-talkie.

Mark gathered up the radio and pressed the transmit button. "Yes," he said in a husky tone.

"We saw you crash into the other boat," Jordan explained. "Are you alright, *Monsieur?*"

"Gaston is dead," the Penetrator replied. "Shot."

There was a pause before Jordan said, "He did not die in vain, Jim. We have won!"

Mark gazed about and discovered the fisherman spoke the truth. The beautiful Caribbean was littered with assorted wreckage and ragged corpse, but ten of the defense fleet boats remained while every yacht and powerboat containing the pirates had been destroyed or captured. Then he saw the tramp steamer in the distance.

"We have to catch up with that cargo ship, Armand," the Penetrator commanded.

"*Comment? Le paquetbot?*" Jordan sounded surprised. "But it is running away, *Monsieur*. . ."

"Armand," Mark cut him off. "I'm not going to let any of these bastards get away."

"We've already lost many boats and even more lives," Jordan protested. "Hasn't there been enough killing?"

"Not quite," the Penetrator replied coldly.

"This is Champmaison," the cop's voice came from the walkie-talkie. "I'm aboard *le Titien*. We'll be there to pick you up so we can follow that *paquebot* and settle with these *couchóns*."

"*Non*," Jordan's voice started. "*Le Voyager* is closer. We will get *Monsieur* Banner while you gather as many more men as you can. I suppose we owe it to Gaston to see this thing through to the end."

"Goddamned right we do," Mark muttered, but all he said into the radio was, "*Merci*, Armand."

18

Cold Cuts

Le Voyager and *le Titien* pursued the fleeing tramp steamer.

The cargo ship moved too slowly to outrun the speedier fishing boats and the last of the pirates on board had but one choice. They had to fight ... and they still had plenty left to fight with.

Three mercenaries manned a .30 caliber machine gun mounted at the stern of the steamer. Despite their inaccuracy from the heaving deck, a murderous volley of slugs cut down three fishermen and two Guadalupian policemen on board *le Voyager*. Bullet-shattered corpse smeared blood on the decks when the impact of the zinging rounds kicked them across the bow of Jordan's boat.

The machine gunners turned their attention to *le Titien* and the Penetrator retaliated with his M-79. His first round fell short and detonated on the surface of the water. His second hit the stern, chipping paint from the ship's name and home port, COMPEADOR—COLÓN. A third 40mm HE grenade sailed into the mercs' position and exploded on the deck. Mangled metal and mutilated bodies were scattered all over the pirate vessel.

Two mercs with a LAW appeared on the fantail, but two of Champmaison's marksmen picked them off before they could use their weapon. More green-clad opponents replaced them and gunfire from rifles and automatic weapons snarled from all three boats. A Soviet-made RPG-7 rocket launcher lobbed an explosive round at *le Titien*. The blast splintered the fishing boat's hull under the bow.

While a pair of mercs reloaded the Russian blaster, a third pirate pulled the pin of a grenade and prepared to hurl it at *le Voyager*, which had just moved within range. The Penetrator acted first.

With a powerful heave, he tossed a black cannister over the high rail of the enemy craft. The concussion grenade rolled toward the nest of mercenaries and exploded. All five pirates on the aft deck were knocked down by the blast and three seconds later, the merc's M-27 frag grenade erupted to rock the steamer once more. Tattered debris, most of it gory chunks of human flesh, fell in a nightmare rain on the decks of *le Voyager*.

A lull followed the carnage, the silence ominous and unsettling, like a midnight stroll through a cemetery only to encounter a headstone with one's name on it. Yet no one stirred on the exposed decks of the pirate's "mother ship." The Penetrator borrowed Armand Jordan's walkie-talkie to contact Champmaison on *le Titien*.

"How's your situation?" Mark inquired.

"Two dead, several wounded," the cop replied.

"The boat is *blesse* as well. We're sinking. Also low on ammunition and completely out of grenades of any kind."

"Okay," the Penetrator began. "Don't try to advance with a leaky boat. Just hang back and wait for Armand to bring *le Voyager* around to pick up your crew."

"*Oui*," Champmaison agreed. "What about the pirate ship?"

"We killed about ten men," Mark replied. "That can't be all of them. I'm going to board her and check to be sure."

"*Etes-vous fou, Monsieur?*" the cop demanded. "Simply blast the boat to Hell. Set fire to it as you did to the others during the battle."

"I'm not sure if I'm crazy or not, Champmaison," the Penetrator answered. "But I don't have any explosives left either and the only way I can set fire to the ship is with a book of matches, so I have to board her. Once everyone is aboard *le Voyager*, come alongside the steamer and follow me. I'll need every gun we've got to back me."

"Why not wait and all go together?"

"There's not enough time," the Penetrator responded. "It would give them a chance to rally and set up defenses. One man, alone might make it to the bridge. If I can cut off the head, the mercenaries can be handled by your man."

"*Zut!*" Champmaison sighed. "We'll try to supply some covering fire for you if those *bastards* appear on deck."

"*Merci*," Mark replied. He handed the walkie-talkie to Jordan. "Are you and your men ready, Armand?"

"*Oui, Monsieur*," the fisherman replied, his

tone suggesting he also doubted the Penetrator's sanity.

Half a dozen armed men aimed their weapons at the cargo ship while the Penetrator slung the Sidewinder over his shoulder. Jordan steered *le Voyager* toward the enemy vessel and eased forward. Mark climbed over the starboard taffrail and watched the port side of the steamer draw closer. He scanned the decks of the *Compeador*. Wreckage, corpses and blood littered the afterdeck, but what about the bow, the bridge or the cabins on the lower decks?

When *le Voyager* was about to touch the steamer, Mark made his move and leaped from the rail. His hands caught a rung of the cargo ship's port ladder. The Penetrator's feet slid along the slick metal hull as he pulled himself higher. Then Mark grabbed the top of the landing platform and easily climbed over it. A short run up the steps brought his head level with the weather rail.

On the enemy's deck, he unslung the Sidewinder and cautiously moved toward the access hatch to the superstructure. Mark felt the steamer shift slightly, which could mean it had been damaged and water was leaking into its belly. Perhaps the remaining pirates were located below deck, making repairs and operating pumps to prevent the *Compeador* from sinking.

Suddenly, he caught a glimpse of movement from the corner of his eye and turned to stare up at the bridge above his head. The movement may have only been the reflection of sunlight on a window . . . or someone lying in wait for him.

The sound of boot leather on steel plate drew his attention to the foredeck, none too soon.

Two mercenaries confronted him. One pointed a Browning Hi-Power at Mark while the other swung up a Uzi submachine gun.

Reflexes, conditioned by years of training and experience, took command of the Penetrator's nerves and muscles. He instantly whipped the Sidewinder toward the pair and opened fire.

A three round burst in the chest pulverized the first merc's sternum and manubrium. Bone splinters accompanied the .45 slugs to do a first-rate demolition job on his heart.

The force of the burst hurtled the hired soldier into his partner who was still trying to bring his Uzi into the melee. The second merc stumbled into the rail when the Penetrator squeezed off another trio of .45 rounds. Heavy hollow-point projectiles turned the merc's face into scarlet pulp and kicked him over the rail for an unscheduled—and permanent—swan dive.

"Uhhhrr!" An inhuman growl erupted behind Mark an instant before something huge and heavy landed on his back.

For a moment, he wondered if somehow the bridge had broken off and fallen on him. Then two arms that could have belonged to a gorilla wrapped around his upper torso, picked Mark up and forcibly hurled him into the weather rail.

The Penetrator connected with the obstacle so hard he almost toppled over it. The violent impact jarred the Sidewinder from his grasp and he watched the submachine gun fall into the ocean below.

Mark pivoted to face his assailant. Bruno smiled and flexed his great fingers in expectation. The Penetrator gazed up at his adversary, astonished by the man's size. Bruno stood almost half a foot taller than Mark and he was built like a bulldozer with arms and legs.

"Awh, hell!" the Penetrator exclaimed, backing away from the giant and trying to draw his MatchMaster.

Mark's fingers and the holstered .45 had been sprayed by sea water. His slippery touch made the draw awkward and Bruno leaped forward before he could finish clearing leather. The brute's powerful fingers closed around Mark's wrist and simply shook the .45 out of his grasp. The Penetrator's free hand delivered a *seiken* fist to the point of Bruno's jaw.

It felt as if he'd tried to punch Mount Rushmore in the mouth.

Steel talons clawed into the top of Mark's head and the brute's other hand caught him under the jaw. One hard twist and the Penetrator's neck would be broken faster than a politician's campaign promises.

Mark's hands flashed to the thick digits of his opponent. They instantly selected a single finger each, grabbd and pulled hard. Bruno grunted in anger and pain as the Penetrator bent the captive fingers backward to the breaking point.

Slowly, Bruno's hands moved from Mark's head and chin. Mark kept applying pressure to the fingers and pushing the monster's arm further apart. Bruno's face contorted in rage, furious that his smaller opponent had managed to get him at a disadvantage. Suddenly, Mark released the giant and drove a hard *empi* to Bruno's jaw and followed with a *shuto* slash for the throat.

The elbow stroke seemed to bounce off the

beast's face without effect and the side of Mark's
hand chopped into a neck muscle. Either blow
would have put a normal man out of action, but
Bruno responded by seizing the Penetrator, picking him up and throwing him like a bale of hay.

Mark sailed seven feet before coming down on
the hard deck. Luckily, he landed on the corpse
of a mercenary which helped to break his fall.
He rolled backward onto the foredeck, toward
the bow. Bruno charged him, head held low like
a fighting bull, ape-like arms extended.

The Penetrator waited for his opponent and
kicked Bruno in the face, feeling the impact
travel up the muscles of his leg. The giant's
charge ceased abruptly and his body jerked
upright, blood spurting from his nostrils. Mark
launched a panther punch for Bruno's windpipe,
but a mallet-sized fist crashed into his face and
propelled him five feet across the deck to the
bow of the steamer.

Mark's body hit the steel plates and rolled
another two feet. Semi-conscious, he found himself sprawled on some thick coils of rope—and
an ominous shadow already draped him like a
black shroud.

Startled, Mark glanced up to see the heavy
wooden shaft of a cargo boom overhead. He
looked around and saw Bruno slowly approach.
Blood ran from his nose to his brutal, smiling
mouth as he wiggled his fingers at Mark, invit-
ing him to get up and continue the fight.

Then the Penetrator spotted a heavy wood-
and-iron pully attached to the end of the rope
beneath him. A block and tackle to the boom, he
realized. Closing both hands around the cable,
he rose slowly, measuring the length of the tackle

and estimating the distance between himself and Bruno.

The giant had become over-confident and stepped closer, failing to see what Mark held until the Penetrator whirled and swung the pully block like an Olympic hammer-thrower. The huge object whistled harshly through the air before it crashed into the side of Bruno's jaw, shattering bone on impact.

Mark watched the blow spin the big man around and rushed forward, lashing out with the block and tackle again. The pully slammed into the back of Bruno's skull and he fell to his hands and knees. The Penetrator viciously flogged his opponent twice more with the improvised weapon, pounding him across the head and between the shoulder blades. Bruno crashed to the deck, flat on his face.

The Penetrator quickly knelt on the giant's back and wrapped the tackle around Bruno's neck. Remarkably, the hulk began to stir. Mark lodged his knee against Bruno's spine and pulled the rope with all his might. His opponent struggled for almost a full minute, nearly bucking Mark off his back. Then, suddenly, Bruno lay still. An ugly gurgle escaped from the man's crushed throat, but Mark continued to strangle the brute until he smelled the stench of urine and feces when the corpse voided itself.

Breathing hard, the Penetrator rose on unsteady legs and walked to his MatchMaster. He picked up the pistol and thumbed off the safety catch. He couldn't account for why no one had taken advantage of his preoccupation with Bruno to put a bullet in him. Wearily, the Penetrator moved to the port side and lowered the landing stage for *le Voyager*, which came leaping up to the steamer.

Quickly the small force of defenders boarded the coastal tramp. Grimly silent they received Mark's instructions and spread out, fore and aft to cover every hatchway and ladder. Sporadic gunfire erupted here and there when the avenging islanders encountered pockets of resistance from the desperate mercanaries. Satisfied that his boarding party had the majority of the enemy bottled up below decks, the Penetrator sent Champmasion and three men to the bridge, while he approached the superstructure to gain access to the cabins inside.

A ship is never truly silent. Water against the hull creates a monotonous creaking sound even if the vessel is otherwise quiet. The Penetrator heard the thud-thud-thud of the steam turbine engine and the whirling hum of a diesel generator when he descended a short flight of steps and entered a dimly lit companionway.

Cabin doors flanked both sides of the narrow hallway. Mark moved to the edge of the first door and kicked it open with the back of his heel, keeping his body clear to the entrance in case a shot replied to his actions. The precaution proved unnecessary because the cabin was empty.

He repeated the procedure at three more doors and found each room unoccupied. Mark prepared to check number five when a shadow danced at the end of the corridor. The Penetrator saw the movement in time and jerked away before pistol shots exploded and bullets ripped into the wall where he'd been a moment before.

Running in a low crouch, Mark dashed to one

of the cabins he had already checked and dove inside as two more slugs splintered the doorframe above his hurtling body. Mark peered around the edge and saw two men at a corner by the end of the companionway. He recognized the wiry, bearded pirate commander, but he didn't know the short fat man with Joe Linsey had actually masterminded the entire operation.

The Penetrator fired back at the pair, his Safari Arms .45 bellowing within the confines of the ship. His bullet scraped steel at the corner near Linsey's whiskers and both he and Kimberly McCulley drew back from view. Linsey's P-38 barked again and a 9mm pellet struck the wall near the cabin. Mark blasted two more rounds at the enemy's position to pin them down and then leaped across the corridor, hitting a door boot-first.

His kick broke the latch and the door popped open, allowing Mark to jump into the cabin. McCulley, holding the long Colt he'd taken from the late Col. Jacoby, wasted two .38 bullets firing at the cubicle Mark had been in before. From his new position, the Penetrator snapped off a shot at McCulley. The .45 round barely missed the top of the fat man's head.

Kimberly McCulley panicked. Unaccustomed to doing his own fighting, he suddenly bolted to a door opposite the position he and Linsey had selected for their attempted ambush. His obese, awkward body made an excellent target when he galloped into the open, but the Penetrator hadn't expected such an opportunity to present itself and he'd ducked back into the cabin after firing a round at McCulley.

Mark saw the pear-shaped criminal's rapidly

waddling figure and hastily squeezed off another shot. McCulley managed to open the door and leaped inside to avoid another slug. The .45 projectile drilled a ragged hole into the door jamb above a hinge as McCulley vanished from view.

Joe Linsey cautiously peered around the corner with his Walther P-38 held ready, hoping to catch the Penetrator off guard after his last shot. To his delighted surprise, he noticed the slide of Mark's pistol had jacked back and locked open after ejecting the final cartridge casing from the weapon's magazine.

Although not the least bit pleased, Mark had been equally surprised to discover his Match-Master was empty after only five rounds. Then he realized that he'd failed to count the two bullets he'd fired into a pirate after Gaston's death. The Penetrator cursed himself for such carelessness and ejected the spent magazine.

Linsey didn't give him a chance to replace it with a fresh mag. The bearded hood had immediately run into the corridor and thurst his P-38 at the Penetrator's face.

"Drop the gun, Hardin!" he ordered, his finger taut on the trigger of the Walther.

Mark bent over and placed the MatchMaster on the floor with one hand while the other plucked a Guardfather from his shirt pocket. He rose slowly, resisting the natural instinct to react quickly in the face of death. Mark mentally assured himself that he still had a chance because his opponent could have shot, but hadn't, which meant an opportunity to survive may yet exist.

"How do you know my name?" the Penetrator asked, folding his arms akimbo on his chest to conceal the Guardfather. The push-button "ice-pick" was a useful weapon, but what sort of chance did it give him against a man armed with a 9mm pistol? The only one he had.

"Vietnam," Linsey declared with a smile. Although he clearly enjoyed his triumph, the hijacker realized he couldn't make any mistakes with the Penetrator and kept six feet between himself and his captive, fearful of a sudden kick or grab for his P-38. "I was part of that black market ring you fucked up for us, but I was in the Navy so they never knew I was involved."

"The Navy?" Mark inquired, stalling for time.

"It's a long story, Hardin," Linsey chuckled. "All I want you to know before I kill you is that I'm the guy that blew the whistle on you and got those army guys to trap your ass in that warehouse in Saigon. They were supposed to have killed you."

"They came close," Mark answered, his thumb braced on the pocket-clip of the Guardfather.

"I'm gonna come a lot closer," Linsey grinned. "Bye-bye, Penetrator . . ."

Mark had only one choice of action and nothing to lose if it failed. He pressed the Guardfather's button and heard the blade snap into place as he unfolded his arms, hurling the weapon at Linsey.

The Walther P-38 roared, but Mark had already thrown himself backward the instant the Guardfather had left his hand. A 9mm round sizzled above the Penetrator's falling body. Linsey screamed and staggered backward into a door jamb across from the Penetrator's cabin. The Walther cracked again, but the bullet struck the deck plates between Linsey's feet, screaming off in a ricochet.

Mark rose swiftly and saw his opponent leaning against a bulkhead, pistol pointed at the deck, eyes and mouth open wide in pain and astonishment. The Guardfather had struck point-first and dangled from Linsey's lower chest. The Penetrator rushed forward and quickly *shuto* chopped the P-38 out of Linsey's grasp. The hood reached for the handle of the Guardfather with his other hand and tried to pull it out of his chest.

The heel of Mark's palm slammed into it first, driving the spike-blade upward, through the solar plexus and into Linsey's heart. The Penetrator rammed a knee into Joe Linsey's groin and and hoped he had lived long enough to feel it. Then he shoved the hijacker's corpse aside and retrieved his MatchMaster pistol.

The Penetrator shoved a fresh magazine into the Safari Arms .45 and moved down the companionway to where the little fat man had fled. He began to appreciate the strain he'd been under since he'd left New Orleans. Seldom had a mission required so much, so quickly. Racing to Honduras and then to Guadalupe, the desperate effort to prepare to combat the invasion, the sea battle and the death of Gaston followed by the punishing fight to the death with Bruno and the nerve-racking confrontation with Linsey—all combined to leave him physically and mentally exhausted.

Mark accepted the fact that he wasn't functioning at peak level as he approched the door Kimberly McCulley had bolted to. He warned himself not to get careless and gently eased the door forward with his foot.

Inside he saw a small mess hall with wooden tables and benches bolted to the floor. He also surmised the location of his quarry. McCulley had to be hovering behind the stainless steel serving counter that divided the mess from the galley. Dumb bastard, Mark thought.

"It's over now," he called out, discovering his voice to be as tired and wrung out as he felt. "Throw out your gun and surrender!"

The Penetrator wasn't surprised when he saw the muzzle of the fat man's revolver poke over the edge of the counter. He jumped away from the door before a .38 slug punched a hole through it. Then he heard the click-click of a hammer striking an empty chamber.

Suspecting a trick, Mark crouched low and shoved the door open with one hand while he quickly fired a .45 round into the steam table McCulley had hidden behind. The fat man cried out in alarm when the 185 grain projectile splintered steel near his head and easily ripped through his "shield."

"Next one goes in your gut!" Mark warned.

Kimberly McCulley rose slowly, arms held high, one pudgy hand fisted around the barrel of the empty Colt revolver. Only then did Mark enter the mess hall.

He approached the last of the pirates. The idea that the fat little man before him had been a pirate, a hijacker or a mercenary seemed laughable, but Mark didn't feel up to uttering even a small chuckle. He wearily waved his pistol at McCulley, gesturing for him to move.

"You must be the Penetrator," the fat man

began in a nervous, shaky voice. "I understand you've had problems with the law in the past. Perhaps once you've heard what I've planned to do in Guadalupe, you'll reconsider . . ."

"You mean *you're* the brains behind this business?" Mark stammered. He glared at Mc-Culley. The idea seemed absurd until he noticed the fanatical brilliance in the little man's bright blue eyes.

"They've always laughed at me," McCulley spat with anger, but tears ran down his cheeks. "They won't laugh now . . ."

The Penetrator almost felt sorry for the little man—but too many lives had been lost to excuse the actions of even a mentally unbalanced individual. McCulley's type always wanted everyone to pay for the actions of a few. Mark had met the sort before and could feel little pity for them. They all seemed to have enough for themselves. Bitterness, hurt and mistreatment can be emotionally devastating, as Mark knew from personal experience, but it didn't give anyone a right to make innocent people suffer for the wrongs and slights they had suffered or they, themselves, had committed.

"Nobody will laugh," the Penetrator agreed. "Everyone is going to take you quite seriously. You might not care for it, but they'll take you very seriously. Now . . ."

Kimberly McCulley then proved that he'd learned everything he knew about combat pistol fighting from the late show. He threw the empty Colt at the Pentrator. Mark easily dodged the revolver and watched McCulley bolt through an entrance behind the chow line. He nearly fired into the fleeing man's back, but hesitated. The guy wasn't worth killing. The Penetrator sighed and followed McCulley into the next compartment.

He found himself in a large modern galley, equipped with a butcher's block table complete with an array of knives, cleavers, ladels and long steel forks. The steamer was outfitted to do some mighty fancy meat processing since it featured an electric band saw mounted on a stand for that purpose, in addition to the usual pots and pans one would expect to find in a seagoing kitchen. Mark found McCulley standing between the saw and the meat cutting table, clearly too distraught to know what to do next.

"I won't hunt you down again," Mark warned. "Try to run and I'll shoot you. I'm too tired to . . ."

Suddenly, the ship lurched violently to one side and threw the Penetrator off balance. Mark staggered, though he managed to stay upright, only to see McCulley advance with a rolling pin in his fist.

The comical image of an overbearing wife chasing her harassed hubby with a rolling pin is a product of someone's weird sense of humor. There would be nothing funny, though, about being hit by a thick wooden instrument that can crack a lobster shell or shatter an ox bone. The Penetrator lost any interest in taking McCulley alive and tried to swing the MatchMaster toward the fat man. His weakened condition betrayed him and McCulley struck Mark's forearm, to send the pistol hurtling from his grasp.

The rolling pin stroke had only been a glancing blow. Even so, it convinced the Penetrator that the chubby little fellow he'd almost felt sorry for could easily kill him. McCulley's eyes gleamed like two cobalt marbles in a doughy mask, making it clear that was exactly what he intended to do when he raised the heavy wooden instrument overhead in a two-handed grip.

Mark immediately threw a side-kick to Mc-Culley's flabby belly, knocking the diminutive criminal back into the butcher's table. McCulley's spine connected with the edge of the block and he released the rolling pin to grab the table and retain his balance. The Penetrator's counterattack had, in fact, thrown his own footing off and he fell against the meat saw. His elbow struck a button and the large, jagged-tooth blade whirled into life next to his left forearm.

The Penetrator retreated from the saw to find himself face-to-face with Kimberly McCulley, now armed with a large steel meat clever. The little man's face contorted with murderous rage as he swung the butcher's hatchet in a deadly backhand stroke.

Mark leaped away and fell against a rack of kitchen utensils. Despite repeated jolts of adrenalin, his head began to swim; a combination of the multiple ordeals he'd already experienced and the nightmare situation of confronting a madman armed with a cleaver in a lopsided room. the awkward slant of the floor didn't seem to effect McCulley. He charged forward, cleaver held high, prepared to split his opponent's skull in two.

The Penetrator's fingers closed around the handle of a cast-iron skillet. He raised the utensil in time to meet the descending blade. Metal clanged harshly when the meat axe connected with the frying pan. Mark's free hand punched McCulley in the mouth. The fat man took two steps backward, grabbed the cleaver in both fists and attacked once more.

Mark held his skillet in a two-handed grip and stepped forward to meet McCulley's stroke. The edge of the skillet struck the lunatic's right wrist under the cleaver, breaking bone on impact, then knocked the handle out of his other hand's grasp.

The Penetrator swiftly whirled the iron implement in a low arc and drove it into McCulley's soft midriff. The fat man gasped and doubled up as Mark discarded the skillet, confident he could easily subdue McCulley and restrain him with a pair of plastic riot cuffs. He grabbed the little man's right arm and began to twist it behind his back.

McCulley suddenly resisted, his body twisting and bucking so violently Mark decided he needed to bat the psycho's head into something to calm him down. McCulley nearly broke free, so the Penetrator shoved him toward the nearest available object, face first.

He didn't realize it was the band saw.

MCulley screamed when the blade sliced through his nose and lips. Teeth erupted from gums as the saw cut a path through the mandible and philtrum bones of his jaw. Merciless steel hacked its way into the glabella, located between McCulley's eyes. Orbital bones cracked apart and two blue eyeballs burst forward and exploded on the deck plates like a pair of blood-filled olives. Before the Penetrator could react in any way, the whirring metal belt had carved halfway through Kimberly McCulley's skull.

Mark found the off button and pressed it. The

whirl of the saw ceased with a whine and the Penetrator staggered from the galley, not wishing to glance back at the hideous clump of mangled meat that had formerly been a man. He leaned against a wall in the mess hall and breathed deeply, smelling the stench of death. His clothes were splattered with Kimberly McCulley's blood and shreds of pink flesh. Mark groaned, fell to his knees and vomited.

Dan Griggs frowned, watching Mark Hardin jab a fork into his baked potato and halfheartedly tow a portion of the food to his mouth. The Penetrator had hardly touched the main course, a big, blood-rare T-bone steak. Dan had always thought this was a favorite of Mark's, which is why he'd suggested they meet in *The Round Up*, one of the best steakhouses in Brownsville, Texas.

"Something wrong?" the Justice man inquired. "You don't seem to have much of an appetite, Mark."

"I'll get over it," the Penetrator answered thinly. "I always do."

"Well," Dan began, sipping some red wine. "I got word that the Guadalupe authorities are holding the survivors of Kimberly McCulley's private army for trial. Oh, did I tell you what we found out about McCulley? Wall Street wizard turned crook? Could have had a helluva future if . . ."

"Yeah," Mark acknowledged. "I know."

"Uh-huh." Dan cleared his throat. "Anyway, looks like everybody in the U.S. who was involved in the scheme is either cooling his heels in prison or six feet under. Might be a few left somewhere in Central America, but all the ringleaders are out of the picture for sure. You saw to that."

I saw ... Mark felt his stomach turn. "It's over, right? So let's eat."

"I'm way ahead of you already, buddy," Dan replied. "One thing—don't ever ask me for another Justice Department ID."

"Oh?" the Penetrator responded, cocking one eyebrow. "Did I do something wrong with the last one?"

"You just bent a few laws and broke about fifty others," the Justice Department official answered. "Such as forced breaking-and-entry, assault with a deadly weapon, violation of suspects' rights, use of torture to acquire confessions, a few little things like that."

"Oh, that," Mark allowed with a nod. "Well, I'm sorry about all that, Dan, but it seemed like a good idea at the time."

Griggs sighed with exasperation. "Yeah. At least I managed to get everything removed from our computers in Washington before the shit could really hit the fan. Matter of fact, I came up with a brilliant explanation about what must have happened. See, I figure that nasty old Penetrator must have somehow gotten a hold of same damn good forgeries and hoodwinked all those cops from Galveston to New Orleans."

"I've heard he's a clever rascal," Mark returned, his mood lightening with a grin.

"Yeah," Dan growled. "With a little help from his friends."

"Friends," Mark confirmed, his mind straying from the conversation. He had some very good friends and he owed them quite a lot ... Dan, Professor Haskins, David Red Eagle and Bobby

Reeve to name a few. Yet, there were a couple of others he'd never see again—Clell Brockman and Gaston Arnaud.

He shook his head, aware that he'd endured too much, too recently and needed some time to recover—physically, mentally and emotionally—at the Stronghold. Then, and only then, could he hope to make sound decisions concerning his future. This was something more than the usual post-mission funk and he had to come to terms with it . . . soon. Whether he chose a future as Mark Hardin or as the Penetrator, it didn't seem he could continue to be both and expect to succeed at being either.

"Hell with it." He dropped his silverware on the plate beside his steak. "I'm going to get a doggy bag for this and take it home. Right now all I want is some sleep."

"You look like you need it," Dan agreed. "In fact, you never looked like you needed it so badly before."

Maybe, Mark thought resignedly, it's time to retire after all.

CELEBRATING 10 YEARS IN PRINT
AND OVER 22 MILLION COPIES SOLD!

CHIUN'S OWN BOOK

CHIUN

Want to know more about Chiun and the House of Sinanju?

You can find it all in THE ASSASSIN'S HANDBOOK. Everything. From the history of the House of Sinanju and Chiun's almost-favorite Ung poem to the Assassin's Quick Weight Loss Diet and 37 Steps to Sexual Ecstasy.

THE ASSASSIN'S HANDBOOK also contains an original, never-before published DESTROYER novella: "The Day Remo Died".

Get this one-of-a-kind, hardcover-size trade paperback at your local bookstore, or order it from Pinnacle with the coupon below.

☐ 41-847-7 THE ASSASSIN'S HANDBOOK
$6.95   created by
RICHARD SAPIR and WARREN MURPHY
compiled and edited by Will Murray